Shear
Terror

Books by Dorothy Howell

Haley Randolph Mysteries
HANDBAGS AND HOMICIDE
PURSES AND POISON
SHOULDER BAGS AND SHOOTINGS
CLUTCHES AND CURSES
TOTE BAGS AND TOE TAGS
EVENING BAGS AND EXECUTIONS
BEACH BAGS AND BURGLARIES
SWAG BAGS AND SWINDLERS
POCKETBOOKS AND PISTOLS

Sewing Studio Mysteries
SEAMS LIKE MURDER
HANGING BY A THREAD
SHEAR TERROR

Published by Kensington Publishing Corp.

DOROTHY HOWELL

Shear Terror

Kensington Publishing Corp.
www.kensingtonbooks.com

KENSINGTON BOOKS are published by

Kensington Publishing Corp.
900 Third Avenue
New York, NY 10022

All Kensington titles, imprints, and distributed lines are available at special quantity discounts for bulk purchases for sales promotion, premiums, fund-raising, educational, or institutional use. Special book excerpts or customized printings can also be created to fit specific needs. For details, write or phone the office of the Kensington Special Sales Manager: Attn. Special Sales Department, Kensington Publishing Corp., 900 Third Avenue, New York, NY 10022. Phone: 1-800-221-2647.

Library of Congress Control Number: 2024936520

KENSINGTON and the KENSINGTON COZIES teapot logo Reg. U.S. Pat. & TM Off.

ISBN: 978-1-4967-4045-8

First Kensington Hardcover Edition: October 2024

ISBN: 978-1-4967-4047-2 (ebook)

10 9 8 7 6 5 4 3 2 1

Printed in the United States of America

ACKNOWLEDGMENTS

Many thanks to my editor, John Scognamiglio, for the many opportunities he's given me and for the faith he's shown in my books.

Much is owed to my agent, Evan Marshall, whose guidance and attentiveness have been invaluable.

A huge thank-you to the team at Kensington for their hard work bringing this book to life.

A special thanks to Stacy Howell, Judith Branstetter, Seth Branstetter, Brian Branstetter, and Martha Cooper for their ongoing unfailing love and support, and to William F. Wu, PhD, for his friendship and advice.

Heartfelt thanks to June Cerza Kolf, who rekindled my love of sewing.

And, of course, my thanks to all the readers who've recommended my books to friends and family, emailed, messaged, written reviews, and stayed in touch.

Shear Terror

CHAPTER 1

Like a lot of things I'd found myself doing lately, this had seemed like a good idea at the time.

I shivered as I took another sip from the travel cup I carried. Tomato juice. Yuck.

Few people were out this early in the morning as I walked down Main Street in Hideaway Grove, the touristy town I'd moved to not long ago—something else that had seemed like a good idea at the time. My life in Los Angeles had fallen apart so I'd retreated to Hideaway Grove, where, as a child, I'd spent idyllic summers with my aunt while my university-professor parents traveled to the far recesses of the planet doing research.

Hideaway Grove, with its pastel-colored storefronts and blooming flower boxes, drew tourists from far and wide to enjoy the specialty and antique shops, art galleries, and restaurants. The town had been founded by a bird-watcher, so most of the streets and businesses were named after birds. It was a small, close-knit community, where most everyone knew each other and supported the common goal of welcoming tourists and conventions to keep the town's businesses solvent.

I took another sip of my tomato juice and cringed. Around me, the stores were opening for the day. Merchants swept the sidewalk, set out water bowls for our four-legged guests and chalkboards announcing the day's sale items.

My aunt Sarah had welcomed me when I'd left Los Angeles, allowing me to take up residence in the bedroom I'd lived in as a child. Her home was just off Main Street on Hummingbird Lane. Aunt Sarah had never married and had no children, so she was glad for the company.

I was glad, too. The only problem I'd run into so far was that her dryer had shrunk my jeans. Not much. Really. A tiny bit. Hardly noticeable.

Okay, actually, Aunt Sarah's dryer hadn't shrunk my jeans. It was Aunt Sarah's bakery.

When I'd pulled on my favorite jeans this morning and found myself engaged in a tug-of-war between the waistband button and the buttonhole—while enjoying a blueberry muffin, one of Aunt Sarah's specialties—I'd realized I had to face the truth. I couldn't blame the bakery. It was all me. I had to take action. The best way to do that, of course, was a Google search.

With only a few taps on my cell phone I'd learned that I should be eating and drinking, or avoiding, antioxidants, gluten, processed meats, refined sugars, and a whole list of other things. Not being clear on exactly what all of that meant, I'd grabbed the bottle of tomato juice from the fridge, filled a travel cup I'd found in the cupboard, and left the house feeling pretty darn good about my healthy choice, even though it tasted yucky.

Just ahead on Main Street was Sarah's Sweets, the bakery my aunt had owned for as long as I could remember, where she turned out delicious and exquisitely handcrafted baked goods. She'd been inside for hours now, baking muffins for early-morning customers and filling the day's orders. I helped out when needed, which had led to a lot of sampling, tasting, just trying a quick bite of—well, too many things, as the waistband of my jeans had told me.

"Abbey!"

That's me. Abbey Chandler. And the person on the sidewalk ahead of me calling my name was Brooke Collins.

I don't like her.

"You're up early," Brooke declared, her ever-present fake smile plastered firmly in place.

Brooke had on yoga togs, which she constantly wore even when she wasn't going to a workout class. She was about my age—I'm twenty-four—and she dressed that way to show off her perfect figure.

I forced myself to take another gulp of tomato juice.

She gestured at my travel cup. "Did you stop by the new smoothie shop?"

No way was I getting into the issue of my shrinking pants.

"Mineral water," I said.

"Well, of course," she said. "That smoothie shop is awfully expensive . . . for some people."

Brooke was married to a dentist. They had a young daughter and lived in a newer, upscale tract of homes just outside of town. I'd heard the place was gorgeous. I didn't know; she'd never invited me to her house.

"Got to run," I said.

"That's right. I heard. You're working at the visitor center now."

Another thing about Hideaway Grove was that news, gossip, and even the tiniest whisper of a scandal traveled at the speed of light.

Brooke's smile vacillated between patronization and pity. "Look at you, working a real job. Isn't that sweet."

"Catch you later," I said, and hoped it wouldn't happen, as I walked away.

"Abbey!"

I huffed to hold in my annoyance and turned back to face her.

"I wanted to let you know," Brooke announced. "We're renewing our vows."

I supposed she meant her wedding vows. I'd never met her husband. I didn't even know his name.

"Our anniversary is coming up, so we're planning something fantastic," Brooke declared.

Okay, so maybe I'd finally get invited to her house.

"I might need you to do some minor alterations on the gowns," Brooke said.

What had I been thinking?

"Nothing big," Brooke added quickly. "I know your sewing skills need a lot of improvement."

Just as I was seriously considering popping the lid off my travel cup and dousing her with tomato juice, Brooke gave me a little finger wave and hurried away.

I headed down Main Street again, thoroughly annoyed—partly because I hadn't been able to wear my favorite jeans today and the tomato juice tasted awful—but mostly with Brooke because her assessment of my sewing skills was accurate.

Shortly after moving to Hideaway Grove, I'd found myself heading up a charity project making pillowcase dresses for girls in Africa. At the time, my sewing skills were pretty much nonexistent. I'd converted the storage room in Aunt Sarah's bakery into a sewing studio, invited women to join the project, and it had turned out to be a fun, productive time for everyone involved.

My sewing skills had improved a little, and I'd become known in Hideaway Grove for my willingness to help with whatever sewing projects needed to be done. Since few people owned a sewing machine these days, I was happy to do minor alterations or repairs. Still, I definitely wouldn't be auditioning for *Project Runway* anytime soon.

Along the way, I'd learned to operate a beast of an embroidery machine and had started making tote bags that featured the town's much-loved symbol, the owl, along with cute, clever captions, to sell to tourists at Hideaway Grove's many events and in some of the shops in town. Thanks to my business degree—my one act of rebellion against my academic parents—and with visions of grandeur, I'd then decided to start my own company selling the totes.

All I can say is that it seemed like a good idea at the time.

Main Street dead-ended at the government center. City hall, the courts, the library, the sheriff's station, and other offices were housed there, alongside a hotel and conference center. Stretched out in front of the buildings was the village green, with picnic tables, playground equipment, and a bandstand, where many of Hideaway Grove's civic events took place.

The visitor center, my destination this morning, was also in the complex, situated on the left. The visitor center and the hotel and conference center bracketed the government offices. I'd gotten a part-time job there a few weeks ago—which says something about the tote bag business I'd started—and now spent a portion of my days answering phones, giving tours to site committees, assisting tourists who were lost or had lost something, and just about anything else that needed to be done.

The visitor center wasn't open for business yet, so I circled to the rear of the complex, where a large lot provided parking and space for deliveries. Even back here, Hideaway Grove's welcoming vibe continued, with shrubs, flowers, and shade trees.

No cars were parked near the visitor center. The rest of the lot was pretty crowded, thanks to the offices in the complex that were already open. In the back corner, a trash truck lumbered toward the line of Dumpsters. Cars and trucks roamed the aisles hoping for an up-close parking space. Men and women dressed in suits, armed with briefcases and messenger bags, flowed in and out of buildings alongside folks there to conduct routine business, some of them wrangling small children.

The back door of the visitor center was closed, which surprised me. I was further surprised when I grasped the knob and realized it was locked. The big roll-up door off to my left was also closed.

While I was always on time for work, I was seldom the first to arrive. That distinction went to Eleanor Franklin.

I glanced around thinking I might see her approaching, saving me the trouble of digging the keys from the depths of my tote, but didn't spot her. I blew out a heavy breath and mumbled, "Of all the days for her to be late."

I'd worked a number of jobs throughout my high school and college years, and I'd gotten my dream position with a prestigious marketing company in Los Angeles—which had turned into a nightmare—and I'd found that there was always someone who made it their mission to be the first to arrive. Maybe to impress the boss, get coffee while it was fresh, or go through everyone else's desk. Who knew? But there was always someone. The *someone* at this job was Eleanor.

She was in her sixties, a widow, and most of her family lived elsewhere, so she focused her time and effort on the many civic and charity projects she worked or volunteered for. I'd found her friendly and helpful—always nice when you're new at a job.

Digging for my keys, I scrounged to the bottom of my

tote, over, under, and around way too much stuff. The lid popped off my travel cup and tomato juice sloshed onto my hand.

"Great . . ." I grumbled.

With one last determined dive, I located my keys at the bottom of my tote, unlocked the door, and went inside.

This back area of the visitor center was a huge storage space, sort of like a multi-car garage, off-limits to everyone but employees. It held the tents we used for vendor events in the village green, dozens of white folding chairs, decorations for every holiday and season, and tons of other stuff. The place was so crowded, in fact, that trails had been created through the clutter to get from the front to the back of the room.

Adding to the chaos were giant cardboard boxes, the kind clothing manufacturers used to ship their merchandise from the factory. Since we weren't shipping anything in them, the lids had been cut off. They were huge, about five feet square and four feet deep. Attempting to reach the bottom could easily result in falling in, headfirst.

All the boxes were full. They held items that had been found in town and turned in to the visitor center over the past year. Today, we'd begin sorting through the contents, organizing everything for the upcoming Lost and Found Day.

I wound my way to the employees' tiny bathroom at the other end of the room situated next to what passed for our break area; really, just a fridge, microwave, and a table and four chairs set up in a corner. In the bathroom, I flipped on the light and dumped the rest of the tomato juice down the drain and dropped the travel cup into the sink.

"Oh, my God, you're bleeding!" someone screamed.

I glanced over my shoulder and saw Paige Easton wide-eyed and panicked, standing behind me, outside the bathroom doorway. I hadn't seen her when I walked in so she must have been just minutes behind me. Paige had recently graduated high school. This was her first job.

"Oh, my God. You're bleeding! *Oh, my God!*" Paige yanked her handbag off her shoulder. "Don't worry! I'll call nine-one-one!"

I realized then that she'd seen the tomato juice covering my hand that had now seeped over my wrist and forearm.

"It's not blood," I said. "It's nothing."

"Lie down!" She frantically scrounged through her bag, presumably looking for her cell phone.

Paige was planning to be a dental hygienist.

"No! Don't lie down! Sit up! And put your feet up!"

Fortunately, not an emergency room tech.

"I'm fine." I rinsed off the tomato juice and held up my arm. "See?"

Paige yanked her phone from her bag and held it up triumphantly.

"Look, Paige," I said, raising my arm higher. "Nothing's wrong."

Paige stared and panted, looking back and forth from my arm to my face. Finally, she plastered her palms against her chest and heaved a huge sigh.

"Oh, my God. You scared me," she declared. "I mean, you really scared me."

"I'm okay," I assured her yet again.

Paige remained near the doorway watching me as if she feared some serious illness might yet befall me, still on alert, still clutching her phone.

"Maybe you should go have some coffee, or something," I suggested, nodding toward the break area.

"I can stay. I think I should stay. Just in case. Don't you think?"

"No. Go. I'm fine."

Paige lingered another moment until I gave her the most

reassuring go-ahead head bob I could muster, then walked away. I rinsed the last of the juice out of my travel cup, dried it and my hands with paper towels, and shoved the cup into my tote.

"Where's Eleanor?" Paige called.

"She's not here yet," I said, as I walked out of the bathroom.

"That's weird," Paige said, standing beside the fridge. "Who else is working today?"

"Me. And I'm not weird," Kendall called as she made her way through the trail of clutter and joined us.

Kendall was tall and dark haired like me, making us bookends of a sort for Paige, who was blond and petite. Kendall was about my age, though she seemed older, as if her life had already been weighed down by too many I've-seen-it-all experiences.

"Eleanor isn't here," Paige told her.

"Okay, that's weird, all right," Kendall agreed. "I don't suppose Miss I'm Better Than You decided to grace us with an appearance today."

"You mean Gloria?" I asked, though I was pretty sure I already knew.

"Who else?" Kendall retorted. "You know how she is with that attitude of hers."

I understood Kendall's comment. Gloria Marsh often rubbed her the wrong way.

"She's not here yet," I said.

"She's supposed to be here today," Paige added. "She's on the schedule."

Kendall waved toward the rows of cardboard boxes. "I don't know why we have to do this," she groused.

"It's for Lost and Found Day," Paige said, sounding like her usual perky self. "One of the best days for Hideaway Grove's residents."

"I say, if the tourists that show up all year long haven't got sense enough to keep up with their stuff, then too bad for them," Kendall said.

Part of our job at the visitor center was to make every conceivable effort imaginable to find the rightful owner for each item turned in and return it. When all efforts proved unsuccessful, the item was earmarked for Lost and Found Day. Once a year everything was put on display and offered for sale at ridiculously low prices to the residents of Hideaway Grove, and anyone else who happened to be in town that day.

Before the sale could take place, all the recovered goods had to be sorted, cataloged, and priced. Today, we were working on clothing. We still had to tackle electronics, cameras, totes, handbags, wallets, jewelry, backpacks, and who knew what else.

Kendall frowned at the boxes, as if collecting her mental energy, then said, "Let's get going so we can get finished. I'll get the tables."

She headed for the stacks of folding banquet tables we used to sort the items on.

"Meet you in the middle," I said to Paige.

I went to the box at one end of the first row; she went to the opposite end.

Paige paused in front of her box. "I wonder why Eleanor isn't here. Do you think she's sick?"

"Be nicer if she'd been out late last night partying and was too hung over to get here on time," Kendall said, as she wrestled a table off the stack.

Honestly, I agreed with her. From what I knew, Eleanor's life was quiet, sedate, conservative. She might enjoy a night of kicking up her heels.

"Maybe I should call her," Paige said.

"Suit yourself," Kendall told her.

"I should call her," Paige said. "Don't you think?"

The box in front of me was filled to the top with jackets, coats, and sweaters. I leaned in and scooped up the top layer of clothing with both hands. I froze.

"Abbey?" Paige asked.

I stared into the box and gasped.

"Abbey, don't you think I should call Eleanor?" Paige asked again.

"Don't bother," I managed to say.

Inside the box, amid the jumble of clothing lay Eleanor Franklin, a giant red stain on the front of her shirt, a metal spike in her chest, her eyes open but seeing nothing. Dead. Not just dead. Murdered.

CHAPTER 2

"It was Eleanor? For sure?"

Paige had asked that question a number of times already—at least I thought it was the same question. Hard to tell with all her tearful blubbering.

"Yes, I'm sure," I said, making an effort to remain calm and compassionate, which wasn't all that easy considering I was still pretty rattled myself.

Paige and I, along with Kendall, were in the visitor center's office, a medium-sized room with big windows that faced Main Street, a counter that ran the width of the room with desks set up behind it, and photos and a rack of brochures showcasing all that Hideaway Grove had to offer.

"So, was it a heart attack?" Paige asked between sobs.

After finding Eleanor's body, I'd told Paige and Kendall she was dead. I hadn't mentioned the bloodstain I'd seen on the front of Eleanor's shirt or the metal spike in her chest. I'd just told them to go into the office and wait while I called the sheriff.

"It was, wasn't it? A heart attack?" Paige gulped hard. "I mean, what else could it have been?"

Kendall, more irritated than rattled, apparently, swiped a box of tissues from the front counter and plunked it down in front of Paige.

"Don't you think?" Paige asked her.

"How would I know?" Kendall demanded, flinging out both arms.

Paige yanked tissues from the box and cried harder.

After I'd made sure Kendall and Paige had gone into the front office and closed the door, I'd followed the path through the clutter to the back of the storage room and opened the big roll-up door just as Deputy Owen Humphrey walked up. Great response time, given the sheriff's station was two doors down.

Deputy Humphrey was a big teddy bear sort of guy, maybe thirty, handsome, and exuding the competent, take-charge air expected from a deputy. He was dating the sister of a friend of mine, so I'd seen him socially a few times.

I'd hoped Deputy Zack McKenna would be the first to respond. I knew him well, and a familiar face—especially his—would have gone a long way toward easing my distress.

Once I'd explained what I'd found and showed him Eleanor's body, Owen first made sure I was as okay as I could be under the circumstances, then jumped into action. I'd left him to it and gone into the office. Now, with Paige still wailing, I wondered if coming in here was the right choice. Again, it seemed like a good idea at the time.

"Finally . . ." Kendall mumbled, gazing out the window at Main Street.

Harriet Griffith, who managed the visitor center, approached. She was mid-forties, dark haired, slender, always well put together, always stressed. Kendall must have called her while I was talking to Owen.

Key already in hand, Harriet unlocked the door, strode inside, and locked the door behind her. She swung around and raked the three of us with her gaze.

"What happened?" she demanded.

"Eleanor's dead!" Paige wailed. "*Dead!*"

Harriet's stress level ramped up. She glared at Kendall, then me, as if it were somehow our fault.

"Abbey found her," Kendall was quick to point out.

"And she's dead?" Harriet demanded.

"Yes," I said.

"What happened?"

"She had a heart attack!" Paige sobbed harder. "And she died! In the stockroom! All by herself!"

Harriet's expression hardened. She paused for a few seconds, thinking, then nodded slowly. "It could have been worse."

Maybe she'd missed the part about Eleanor actually dying.

"We'll have to contain this, as much as possible," Harriet declared. "Keep a lid on it, keep it quiet."

Harriet looked even more stressed than usual. She was always stressed because, in large part, the future of Hideaway Grove rested on her shoulders. She'd been hired not long ago to manage what used to be called the tourist bureau—*visitor center* sounded more friendly and welcoming, she'd decided—taking over from Janine, who still worked here and who seemed okay with the change.

That made Harriet the person responsible for drawing tourists and conventions to town that would keep the local businesses afloat, which meant always presenting Hideaway Grove in the best possible light. If the continual influx of new dollars dried up, the store owners suffered, and Harriet not only heard about it endlessly but also faced the consequences—losing her job being the worst.

"Who else knows about this?" Harriet asked.

I could see she'd shifted into damage control mode.

"Just the three of us," I said, and gestured to Paige and Kendall.

"That's good."

Harriet seemed to relax a bit, apparently thinking the news wasn't that bad, just an unfortunate event that would be dealt with and soon forgotten.

It didn't seem like a good time to tell her Eleanor had been murdered.

"And the sheriff," I added, and gestured to the door that led to the storage room.

"Miss I'm Better Than You was supposed to be here," Kendall pointed out.

"Gloria," I explained to Harriet. "Gloria Marsh."

"She didn't show up," Kendall added.

"Gloria is a volunteer," Harriet said, as if that justified her absence and that she was relieved it meant that, so far, no one else knew about Eleanor's death.

"Oh, my God!" Paige's mouth flew open as if a new horror had just occurred to her. "What if it wasn't a heart attack? What if Eleanor fell? What if she tripped on something? Or slipped? And hit her head? And that's why she *died*!"

Harriet moaned and wobbled slightly, likely thinking now that not only could Hideaway Grove's tourists stay away because of Eleanor's death, but she might become embroiled in a negligence lawsuit brought by Eleanor's family.

"Stop making stuff up," Kendall barked at Paige. "You're making things up. Stop."

Paige cried harder and cradled the box of tissues in both arms.

"Paige should go home," I said to Harriet.

"We should all go home," Kendall declared. "We can't work on the lost-and-found things with the sheriff and all those crime techs in the storage room. There's no reason to be here."

"What's on today's schedule?" Harriet asked.

When I'd come to work here, I'd been surprised to see that everything the visitor center managed was recorded manually, as it had been done for decades. Conferences, festivals, site committee tours, most of the lost-and-found items, employees' work and vacation schedules, volunteer hours, everything. The computer that sat on a table at the back of the room largely went unused. The telephones were big, black, chunky things with a row of flashing lights under the keypad, and a curling cord attached to the handset, which everyone called the *receiver*. I was okay with this method of tracking events; at my previous job, the plan for a paperless office had looked really good—on paper.

I grabbed the ancient ledgers and calendar from the top of the filing cabinet and flipped through them.

"Nothing for this afternoon," I reported.

"Good." Harriet sighed with relief, then gasped. "The dish ladies? Aren't they coming today?"

The dish ladies were the site committee for the Society for the Preservation of Elegant Dining who were considering holding their next event in Hideaway Grove. We called them the dish ladies because, well, we didn't know what else to call them. I knew they weren't coming today because I'd been tasked with ushering them around town.

Still, I rechecked the calendar to reassure Harriet.

"They're not due for a while yet," I told her.

"Good. Because they're important. Very important. You know that, don't you?"

Yes, I knew the dish ladies were important because Harriet had told me that a few dozen times already, plus I had good sense.

"And the brides?" Harriet asked, more concerned now.

Hideaway Grove had booked a bridal show at the convention center. I knew nothing was on the schedule for their event, but I looked at the calendar anyway to ease Harriet's distress.

"Nothing soon," I said.

"The sheriff!" Paige swiped at her nose with a handful of mangled tissues. "I can't leave! I'm a witness! Sheriff Grumman will want to talk to me! He'll want to know what I saw!"

I was pretty sure that Paige, in her current condition, would be the very last person Sheriff Grumman would want to deal with at the moment.

Or maybe that was just me.

"If the sheriff wants to talk to any of us, he knows where to find us," Kendall declared.

Paige yowled again. "What if I have to testify!"

Kendall huffed irritably and announced, "I'm taking her home."

Harriet didn't protest, which I was thankful for.

Kendall caught Paige's upper arm. "Come on."

She pulled Paige toward the door, then turned to Harriet. "And I'm not coming back."

Kendall fished her key from her pocket, unlocked the door and left, towing Paige, clutching the box of tissues and still sobbing, behind her.

Neither Harriet nor I spoke for a few minutes, savoring the silence in the room—at least, I was.

"I'll stay," I offered.

Really, I didn't want to be here. I was still shaken from finding Eleanor's body. But the visitor center was expected to open for business shortly. Even though no events were planned for today there would still be phone calls to answer and tourists stopping by.

That wasn't all, of course. Word of Eleanor's death was probably making the rounds through Hideaway Grove already, and business owners and residents would stop by or call, anxious to get details.

Harriet stewed for a moment, then said, "You should go home."

I wanted to go home. But I was reluctant to leave Harriet here alone to face the sheriff, wait out the crime-scene techs, and deal with the public by herself.

"I can stay," I said.

"You've been through a shock," she said. "You should go."

"I don't mind staying. Really."

"No. We'll close for the day. We'll leave the answering machine on and the CLOSED sign on the door." Harriet looked at the door at the back of the office that led to the storage room, and drew herself up. "I suppose I ought to speak with Sheriff Grumman."

For a moment I wondered if I should go talk to him myself. I'd found Eleanor's body. He'd want to question me.

But I figured he was busy with whatever was going on back there with the crime-scene techs and might not appreciate my intrusion. I'd already explained everything to Owen; he hadn't told me to hang around. And if the sheriff was anxious to talk to me, he'd have come in here already and done so.

I decided that Sheriff Grumman would get around to interviewing me sooner or later, and in a town the size of Hideaway Grove, he would know exactly where to find me. I couldn't see a reason to stay—especially since I didn't want to be here.

"Okay, I'll go," I said. "Let me know if you need anything. I can come back. It's no trouble."

Harriet gestured to the front door. "Just lock up when you leave."

I grabbed my tote but waited until Harriet went into the storage room. Tempted as I was to peek through the door when she opened it, hoping to spot Zack, I didn't. Zack and

I had something going—nothing official—but we both felt a connection, even if it didn't seem to be going anywhere yet.

While something about his presence brought me a lot of comfort, I didn't want to take a chance on what else I might see in the storage room. I already had an ugly picture in my head; I didn't want another one.

I left through the front door and locked it behind me. Life seemed to go on as usual, with folks walking their dogs, tourists and locals ducking in and out of shops, cars rolling down Main Street. A quiet, relaxed morning in Hideaway Grove.

If only my morning had been as pleasant.

I dropped the key into my tote and heard a *clank*.

"What the . . . ?"

I peered inside my tote and saw the travel cup I'd used earlier. Seeing it sent an unwelcome flash of images through my head—spilling the tomato juice on my hand while unlocking the back door, annoyed that Eleanor wasn't already here, going inside, chatting with Paige and Kendall, starting the day's work while all along Eleanor lay dead right next to us. And then seeing that spike and the giant red stain on the front of her shirt.

A little wave of nausea went through me, giving me yet another reason to never drink tomato juice again.

I circled the building, determinedly didn't look toward what was going on at the rear of the visitor center, tossed the travel cup into the Dumpster, and dashed toward Main Street.

I needed comfort and Aunt Sarah's bakery was the best place to find it. No matter how my favorite jeans fit.

"What happened?"

"Was it Eleanor? Really?"

"Is she dead?"

The questions started as soon as I walked through the door into Aunt Sarah's bakery. I wasn't surprised.

Gathered in front of the bakery's glass display case were Geraldine, who ran Sassy Fashions next door, and Anna, the owner of Anna's Treasures, the thrift shop located down the street. Aunt Sarah stood behind the case. Farther back was the kitchen with its big work island surrounded by gleaming appliances and spotless cabinets.

"Are you all right?" Aunt Sarah asked.

Though officially a senior now, she looked and acted years younger, and was a welcome sight. There was an air of calm about her, much like the bakery itself with its mint-green walls and accents of pink and yellow. The small white tables and yellow padded chairs by the front windows were empty of customers.

"I'm okay . . . kind of," I said.

Anna was, as always, sensibly dressed for a woman in her mid-forties in elastic-waist pants, a button-up shirt, and flats. She held up her half-eaten sugar cookie.

"Eat something," she said. "You'll feel better."

"Tell us what happened," Geraldine insisted.

Geraldine looked as sassy as the clothing she sold next door. Today she had on a hot-pink belted dress that clung to her curves, and matching three-inch pumps. Though rumored to be over forty, she'd never admitted it.

"Eleanor was found dead at the visitor center this morning," I said.

All three of them gasped.

"I heard she had a heart attack," Anna said.

"So young?" Aunt Sarah said.

Geraldine ran her hands down her hips. "That's why I take such good care of myself. I'm sure you've noticed. Everybody does."

"Eleanor must have been in her sixties," Anna pointed out.

"Still too young to die," Aunt Sarah said.

"Maybe it was a stroke," Anna said, taking another bite of the cookie.

"It was a fall," Geraldine insisted. "I heard she fell and hit her head."

I didn't correct them. I didn't want to get into it and be reminded of everything I'd seen earlier.

"The sheriff and crime-scene techs were still there when I left," I said. "Harriet decided we should close for the day."

"Who else was there?" Aunt Sarah asked.

"Paige and Kendall. Paige took it pretty hard," I said. "Gloria was supposed to be there this morning, but she didn't show up."

"I'm not surprised," Geraldine said, pursing her lips in disgust. "She does what she wants, regardless."

"She's just trying to find her way, now that she's alone," Aunt Sarah said.

"Playing the widow card doesn't sit right with me," Geraldine said.

"Harriet was really stressed," I said. "I told her I'd stay until the sheriff finished, but she said she could handle it alone."

"I guess we'll have to wait to find out what really happened," Geraldine said.

Neither Geraldine nor Anna looked as if it suited them to wait. Finally, Geraldine shrugged.

"I'd better get back to the shop," she said.

"Me too," Anna said. "New stock to sort through."

Anna popped the last of the sugar cookie into her mouth and followed Geraldine out the door.

Aunt Sarah came around the display case and gave me a

hug. She'd always been my rock, my anchor, since the first summer I spent with her when I was seven. Even though she had no children, somehow she always knew the right thing to say and do to make me feel better.

"Thanks," I said.

Behind us in the kitchen, a timer buzzed.

"Let me know if you want to talk," Aunt Sarah said.

She gave me a gentle smile and went back around the display case and into the kitchen. I lingered for a moment, then crossed the room, opened the pocket doors, and went into the sewing studio.

Morning sunlight beamed through the windows that faced Main Street, muted by the old-fashioned roll-up shades, highlighting the rack of pillowcase dresses ready to be shipped, the design board pinned with fabric swatches, the sewing machines lined up on tables that the volunteers used during our pillowcase dress parties, the embroidery machine I'd finally learned to use, and the stack of tote bags I'd made for my business that wasn't exactly flourishing.

I ambled through the sewing studio, putting things away, straightening up, sorting through spools of thread and lace. There were a number of projects that needed my attention. I couldn't seem to focus. Images of the storage room at the visitor center kept playing in my head, like a terrible movie I couldn't stop.

A familiar voice drifted in from the bakery causing my heart to beat a little faster. A few seconds later, Deputy Sheriff Zack McKenna walked into the sewing studio.

Tall, broad shouldered, athletic, dark hair, handsome. He wasn't in uniform. Off duty, apparently. Hideaway Grove's sheriff department was small, so I wondered if Zack had been notified and gone to the crime scene regardless of his duty schedule. I wondered, too, if Owen had called him with the news that I'd been at the visitor center and found Eleanor's body.

Everything about Zack made me melt a little. Doubly so, now that he'd come to check on me.

Or maybe something else was going on.

Zack didn't rush to me, take me in his arms, attempt to comfort me or ask how I was holding up. He lingered near the pocket doors, a decidedly uncompassionate expression on his face.

"What can you tell me about scissors?" he asked.

Talk about lacking compassion. I was stunned—and hurt. Owen, whom I barely knew, had been kind and caring at the crime scene. Zack and I had a little something going—and *this* is how he treated me?

Zack waved his hand around the sewing studio.

"Scissors," he said. "You use scissors. What kind?"

"That's why you came here? Now? To ask about scissors?"

My words came out sounding harsh because that's how I meant them.

"Go ask Connie," I told him. Connie owned the fabric store down the street.

"I'm asking you," Zack said. "Are there different kinds?"

Exasperated, I huffed. "Yes. Of course. Scissors have blades shorter than seven inches. Anything longer is called shears. Pinking shears, tailor's shears, dressmaker shears, garden shears, all kinds of shears."

Zack listened, intense, nothing like the calm and patient mode he usually displayed. He nodded slowly, his gaze harsh.

"Dressmaker shears," he said. "You own dressmaker shears?"

"Of course I own—" I stopped. "What's going on?"

"Eleanor Franklin was murdered." Zack touched his palm to his chest over his heart. "With dressmaker shears."

The metal spike I'd seen impaled in Eleanor was shears? I hadn't looked closely enough—hadn't wanted to look closely enough—to realize that's what it was.

But now I realized something more, something worse, and it stopped me cold.

The implication hit me like a tidal wave.

"And you think—"

"—the sheriff thinks," Zack said.

"—that I murdered Eleanor? Are you serious? That's crazy. There must be hundreds of pairs of shears in Hideaway Grove. Why would the sheriff possibly think it was me?"

"The shears, the ones used to murder Eleanor . . ."

Zack paused. Now I saw past his intense expression. Now I saw the worry and concern beneath it. Now I got scared.

He drew a breath and tried again.

"The shears used to murder Eleanor are engraved with your name."

CHAPTER 3

Zack lingered near the pocket doors, watching me, waiting. I suppose he expected me to say something that would explain why a murder weapon had my name engraved on it. But I couldn't form a coherent thought. It didn't make sense.

"Sheriff's going to want to talk to you," he said.

I managed to nod.

"I've got to get over there," he said.

I realized then that Zack had put his job in jeopardy by coming to me, telling me about the shears, giving me a heads-up, an advance warning. If Sheriff Grumman found out he'd done that, it wouldn't go well for him.

I guess I should have been grateful. And I was. Really. But at the moment it was just another emotional blow.

Zack waited another minute, then left. I stared after him, unable to move. Finally, I turned around and wandered aimlessly through the sewing studio, trying to make sense of everything.

All I could picture in my head was Eleanor lying in that

bin of clothing, with the big bloodstain on her shirt. I'd been so stunned, I hadn't even noticed that the spike in her chest was a pair of shears.

"Abbey?"

I whirled around and saw Caitlin Patterson rush through the pocket doors, a worried expression on her face.

"Are you okay?" she asked.

Tall, blond, a little older than me, Caitlin had been my best friend during my childhood summers in Hideaway Grove. When I'd moved back, we'd reconnected as if no time had passed.

"I heard what happened," she said.

Caitlin's dad owned Barry's Pet Emporium across Main Street, and she worked there. Her dad had struggled with health problems for a while now, so most everyone kept bad news from him, fearing it could trigger another heart attack. If Caitlin's dad had heard about Eleanor's death, it was already all over town.

"How's your dad?" I asked. "He heard?"

"I'm afraid so."

"How's he taking it?"

"The usual. Ranting. Stressed. Going on and on about the demise of Hideaway Grove, crime, the sheriff," Caitlin said. "But how about you? I heard you were there. Are you okay?"

"No. Not really," I admitted.

"Sit down." She pulled two of the folding chairs away from one of the tables that held the sewing machines, and we sat. "It must have been awful, being there, knowing what had happened."

"Kendall and Paige were there, too," I said.

"Paige?" Caitlin shook her head. "She must have totally lost it."

"Yep," I said.

I explained that Kendall had taken Paige home and that when Harriet arrived, she'd decided to close the visitor center for the day. I told her that I was the one who'd found Eleanor's body.

"What a terrible thing for you to have to go through." Caitlin slid her arm around my shoulders and gave me a quick squeeze.

She didn't ask for details, thankfully. I didn't want to talk about it.

"I saw Zack leave the bakery a few minutes ago," Caitlin said. "He came to check on you. That was sweet of him."

Nor did I want to talk about Zack's real reason for coming here.

"Harriet must have been upset—more so than usual," Caitlin said.

"She's always worried she'll lose her job if a big event cancels," I said. "Can't say that I blame her."

"What's coming up?"

The visitor center always notified the merchants of scheduled events so they could plan a sale or order additional or specialty stock. Caitlin's dad rarely participated.

"Lost and Found Day," I said. "The site committee for the dish ladies, then the bridal show."

"Sheriff Grumman should have Eleanor's death handled by then, since it was a heart attack—"

Caitlin's cell phone buzzed. She pulled it from the pocket of her jeans, saw the name on the ID screen, and groaned.

"Sorry," she said to me, then answered the call. She listened for a minute. "Okay. I will. Right now."

Caitlin ended the call. "I've got to get back to the store."

Her dad was adamant that Caitlin take over the pet store if he ever actually went through with his retirement plans, and he expected her to be as devoted to the business as he was.

"Let's get together later, okay?" she said.

"I'd like that," I called as she hurried out of the sewing studio.

I sat there for another minute or so, gathering my energy. I had things to do, and staying busy would surely be best for me.

Still, I sat there a while longer thinking about—and dreading—the arrival of Sheriff Grumman. He'd show up with questions about my involvement in Eleanor's murder, which I knew wouldn't go well.

When I'd arrived in Hideaway Grove, the sheriff and I had gotten off to a bad start when we'd tangled over the death of one of the town's finest citizens. Things between us had never improved. He didn't like me. I didn't like him, either.

I knew he already suspected me in Eleanor's death. I knew his questions would be harsh, threatening, demanding. But what could I possibly tell him? I had no idea how shears engraved with my name had fallen into the hands of a murderer.

Forcing myself out of my chair, I went to the small bin in the center of one of the tables. Inside the bin lay an array of scissors, shears, seam rippers, and bobbins the volunteers used at our pillowcase dress parties. I kept plenty of each on hand, and people graciously made donations.

There, in the jumble of items, lay shears engraved with my name. They'd been a gift—an expensive gift—from Gloria Marsh, one of the volunteers at my pillowcase dress parties and at the visitor center. Her donation hadn't gone over well with everyone, but, still, the shears were excellent quality, and I was glad to have them.

Gloria had donated four pairs. Three pairs were in the bin. A little wave of anxiety went through me, thinking where the fourth pair was at this moment.

I closed my eyes for a few seconds and heard a moan slip

through my lips. What was I going to say when Sheriff Grumman confronted me?

A voice drifted in from the bakery. Sheriff Grumman? Panic set in. I didn't want to talk to him. He was already convinced I was involved in Eleanor's death, according to Zack. I was a suspect—his only suspect. He might actually arrest me.

No way was I waiting around for that to happen. I had to escape.

Frantic, I looked around, even though I knew there was only one functioning exit from the sewing studio. The big windows that faced Main Street were as old as the building, reaching almost from the floor to the ceiling, and sills wide enough to use as a shelf. With wooden frames, warped by time and weather, the windows were almost impossible to lift. That meant the only way out was through the bakery.

I'd have to make a run for it, I decided, through the bakery and out the rear door that opened into the alley. The sheriff was in his fifties and not exactly in great shape. I could outrun him.

I edged closer to the pocket doors and listened harder. A woman's voice. I nearly collapsed with relief.

Peering into the bakery I spotted Harriet at the display counter talking to Aunt Sarah.

"Is the sheriff finished at the visitor center already?" I asked as I walked over.

"He's gone, thank goodness," Harriet said.

She looked tired, worn down, and frazzled. Maybe I should have insisted on staying with her at the visitor center.

"Gloria finally showed up asking all sorts of questions. I think she's been watching too many crime shows on TV since her husband died," Harriet said. "The deputies and those techs are still there, but Sheriff Grumman left. Has he been here to see you yet?"

I shook my head hoping I didn't look as if I'd just contemplated bolting from the bakery to avoid being questioned.

"He talked to Paige," Harriet said. "She called me afterwards, a hysterical mess."

"She's very sensitive," Aunt Sarah said.

"And Sheriff Grumman can be intimidating." Harriet frowned. "Though why he's carrying on as if this is some sort of crime, I don't know. Poor Eleanor. Bad enough her heart gave out. Why try to turn it into something more?"

I knew it was, in fact, something more. Everyone in Hideaway Grove would find out before long.

Harriet drew a breath. "So, I decided I'd had enough, and I left. Except for . . . this."

"A muffin basket for Eleanor's niece," Aunt Sarah explained. She must have seen the confused look on my face, and said, "Rayna Newberg. She works across the street at Birdie's Gifts and Gadgets."

Even though I'd lived in Hideaway Grove for a while now, I still didn't know all the town's intricate connections.

"I'll get this basket for you now," Aunt Sarah said, and went back into the kitchen.

"Does Eleanor have other family in town?" I asked.

"Just Rayna." Harriet squeezed her eyes shut for a few seconds and pinched the bridge of her nose. "I feel I have to do this but, honestly . . ."

"I'll deliver it," I said.

I didn't want to talk to the sheriff. He knew he could find me here at the bakery or at home. What better way to avoid him?

Harriet hesitated for a few seconds. "No. Thank you. I really should do it myself."

"Let me," I said. "I'll explain that you've been tied up with the sheriff. She'll understand."

Harriet frowned and looked hard at me. "You'll deliver it right away?"

"Of course."

"Because it's important. Very important. You understand that, don't you?"

"Absolutely."

Harriet continued to stare at me as if judging my ability to handle what I considered a mindless task.

"I'll handle it," I assured her.

She drew a heavy breath.

"Don't worry," I said.

"Well, all right. Thank you. I really would like to go home and lie down."

"You should get some rest," I said.

"Rayna lives in the yellow house on Dove Drive, across from the apartments."

No address needed, no GPS required, no turn-by-turn directions necessary, just the bare-bones description Harriet had given. Life in a small town.

"She's home," Harriet said. "I already checked."

Harriet lingered for a moment, still staring at me, still, apparently, judging my competence to walk three blocks and ring a doorbell. I fought the urge to glance outside for Sheriff Grumman's approach and, finally, Harriet called her thanks to Aunt Sarah and left the bakery.

I went into the kitchen as Aunt Sarah was wrapping a basket of a dozen muffins in cellophane. Instead of the bakery's usual pastel colors, she tied it with a somber brown bow.

"Where's Jodi?" I asked.

I'd been so rattled I hadn't noticed that Aunt Sarah's part-time assistant wasn't there.

"She had an appointment," Aunt Sarah explained.

"I'll be back as soon as I can, in case you get busy," I said.

"Give Rayna my condolences."

I took the basket, slipped into the sewing studio and retrieved my tote bag, then closed the pocket doors and left the bakery. Outside, I checked the street in both directions. No sign of the sheriff. Still, if I was going to avoid him, there was no sense in parading myself down Main Street.

Dodging traffic, I darted across the street, then slipped into the alley that ran between Birdie's and the pet store. I paused at the rear of the buildings and leaned around the corner. Another alley ran behind the stores just wide enough for customer and employee parking and delivery vans. A few people were there. No sign of Sheriff Grumman.

A ball of orange fluff jumped out at me. I swallowed a yelp, froze, and saw Hideaway Grove's apparently homeless cat staring up at me. Cheddar had the run of the town, appearing and disappearing at will, and turning up at odd times.

Cheddar seemed to be on high alert, meowing and turning in a circle, as if he somehow knew I was up to something.

"Don't tell anybody you saw me," I whispered.

Cheddar meowed again and trotted away.

Though I was hardly inconspicuous carrying a huge basket of muffins tied with a giant bow, I moved as stealthily as possible down the alley, crossed Eagle Avenue and Blue Bird Lane, and turned down Dove Drive. Just as Harriet had told me, I easily spotted Rayna's house.

Like all towns and cities, some neighborhoods held up better than others. This end of Dove Drive hadn't fared well. Rayna's house, which at some point must have been painted a cheery yellow, had faded to a dull beige. Several planks in the picket fence were missing, and the yard it surrounded displayed more weeds than grass and flowers.

I didn't worry that I might run into Sheriff Grumman. He would have come here first to notify Eleanor's niece of her death. Still, on the off chance he'd circled back for some reason, I held the basket of muffins higher, blocking my face, and peeked around it as I approached Rayna's front door.

She opened the door almost immediately after I rang the bell. I recognized her from the times I'd seen her at Birdie's Gifts and Gadgets. Rayna was mid-thirties, trim, with short dark hair, neat, tidy, though it was clear she didn't have her hair or nails professionally done or go in for makeup or expensive clothing. Rayna was pleasant looking, usually. Not now.

Her eyes were red, her cheeks were flushed, and tears slid down her face. She clutched a handful of tissues.

"I'm so sorry about your aunt." I jiggled the muffin basket. "This is from the visitor center."

"The visitor center!" Rayna drew a great ragged breath and sobbed. "That's where she was killed—and it's all my fault!"

CHAPTER 4

"We argued!" Rayna wailed harder. "Eleanor and I. We argued."

We were in Rayna's kitchen. No one else was in the house for what I thought might be her confession to her aunt's murder.

The kitchen, like the rest of the house that I'd seen, was clean, tidy. No dishes sat in the sink, no crumbs were on the countertops. A mudroom with the washer and dryer led to the door that opened into the backyard, which was mostly weeds.

I placed the muffin basket on the dinette table. Rayna didn't seem to notice.

"All we had was each other." Rayna yanked another tissue from the box clamped under her arm. "Family. We were family. Just the two of us living here in town, and . . . and . . ."

She sobbed and clutched the tissue in her fist, hardly looking like someone who was trying to confess to a murder. Still, something had happened between the two of them. If it had been a situation that had gone too far, I didn't want to miss what she was confessing to.

"So, you two argued?" I asked, trying to keep her talking.

Rayna nodded and swiped her nose with the tissue. "Yes."

"About what?" I asked.

She gulped hard, assessed the crumpled tissue in her hand, then dropped it into the trash can beside the stove.

"Eleanor was a crusader," Rayna said. "She always had some sort of cause she cared about."

"I didn't know her very well," I said.

Rayna reached for another tissue, saw the box was empty, and tossed it into the trash can.

"Oh, yes. She had a strong sense of right and wrong," Rayna said.

"And that's what you argued about?" I asked.

"I'm afraid so." Rayna swiped at her tears with the back of her hand, then pulled a paper towel off the roll next to the sink.

"What, exactly, happened?" I asked.

She retrieved the empty tissue box from the trash can and stuffed the paper towel into it.

"My rent," Rayna said.

I didn't know Rayna rented her house but wasn't surprised.

"The *rent!*" Another torrent of emotion hit her. She pulled the paper towel from the tissue box and held it to her face as she cried.

Honestly, I was having trouble following what Rayna was trying to tell me—or, perhaps, confess.

"Your aunt lived here? With you?" I asked.

Rayna sniffed hard and gestured to the back of the house, the paper towel clutched in her hand. "She lives behind me. Through the block. On Blue Bird Lane."

"You rented this place from Eleanor?" I asked.

"No." Rayna shook her head. "The landlord raised my rent. Eleanor said I should refuse to pay it. Easy for her to say. She owns her home. And she was right, kind of. I mean, look at this place. It's not in the best shape. I know that. But what am I supposed to do? Move? I can't afford to move. And where would I go? Could I even find a place to rent here in town?"

Since I'd returned to Hideaway Grove, I'd considered moving out of Aunt Sarah's house and getting a place of my own. I'd faced the same situation as Rayna. Moving meant coming up with a deposit and first month's rent—a big chunk of money. Plus, there weren't a lot of places available for rent in town.

"She meant well." Rayna blew her nose on the paper towel, then dropped it in the trash can. "Eleanor, she meant well. I know she did. But I couldn't take her advice. Just refuse to pay the rent increase? And then what? Get evicted?"

"That's a tough choice," I said.

Rayna sniffed and was quiet for a few seconds.

"Maybe I should have done as she asked. Maybe if I hadn't disagreed, she'd still be alive," she said softly. "That's why . . . that's why I think it's my fault!"

Rayna's sobs ramped up again. She swiped the dish towel hanging on the handle of the oven door and pushed it into the tissue box.

"Why do you think it's your fault?" I asked.

"She was upset with me because I wouldn't go along with what she wanted me to do. She left. She didn't even finish her coffee!" Rayna pulled the dish towel out of the tissue box and wiped her tears with it. "Maybe . . . maybe if she'd stayed here longer, if she hadn't gotten to the visitor center when she did, things would have turned out differently. Maybe she wouldn't have been killed."

"Do you have any idea who'd want to murder her?"

"No." Rayna shook her head. "The sheriff asked me that, too."

"Did he tell you if he'd found a suspect?" I held my breath, waiting for her answer.

"No."

I started breathing again, relieved Sheriff Grumman wasn't blabbing my name all over town—yet.

"It must have been someone trying to rob the visitor center," she said.

"Did the sheriff tell you that?"

"Not exactly. Well, kind of," Rayna said. "I mean, it must be the reason, don't you think? I told him I couldn't think of anyone—anyone—who'd want to hurt Eleanor. Everybody loved her. Everybody!"

Well, not everybody, I thought.

Rayna dabbed her eyes again with the dish towel, then blew her nose on it.

"Eleanor was a good person. She was always volunteering and helping with things in town," Rayna said.

"Eleanor came to the sewing studio for the pillowcase dress parties," I said.

Rayna wiped her nose again on the dish towel, then hung it back on the handle of the oven door.

"She donated those scissors," Rayna pointed out.

Eleanor, like many others in town, had donated to the pillowcase dress charity. She'd purchased a half dozen pairs of scissors and left them at the sewing studio for the volunteers to use. They were good scissors—I appreciated the gesture—even though her generosity ended up causing what turned out to be an ongoing headache.

"If somebody had a problem, she was always there to lend an ear and offer advice," Rayna said.

"Like the situation with your rent?"

"Exactly. She always encouraged people to do the right

thing. She had a point. There was no reason for the rent increase. Nothing had been improved here, so how could she justify the increase?" Rayna shook her head, looking around her kitchen. "I don't know how I'm going to pay more rent. I can barely make ends meet now. You know how it is."

I did know, and it wasn't a good feeling.

"Eleanor wasn't close with her children—her stepchildren, really. She was my aunt, but more like a good friend. I loved her." Rayna pressed her lips together for a moment, as if trying to hold in her emotions. "But sometimes she'd make me so mad. So mad I could hardly see straight."

I wondered just how mad that could be.

"What happened after you two argued?" I asked.

"Nothing. She left." Tears pooled in Rayna's eyes again. "That's the last time I saw her."

The doorbell rang. Rayna looked lost for a moment, then left the kitchen. I grabbed the dish towel from the handle of the oven door, stepped into the mudroom and threw it into the dirty laundry basket, then washed my hands at the sink.

When I got to the living room, I saw that the mayor had arrived. Margaret Green was fiftyish, with a hairstyle that should have been updated decades ago, dressed conservatively. She'd come to pay her respects, which was expected from the mayor of a small town. I exchanged a few words with her, then left.

I stopped outside and pressed my back against Rayna's front door. My gaze swept the street, looking for Sheriff Grumman. Hopefully, he was somewhere else looking for Eleanor's killer, but he might have doubled back and come here. I leaned forward a bit judging the distance to the alley that I could cut through and estimated how quickly I could get there unseen.

Then I stopped. What was I doing? Why was I acting this way? Why was I hiding from the sheriff? I hadn't done anything wrong. Just because Eleanor had been murdered with shears engraved with my name, it didn't mean I was responsible. The shears weren't kept under lock and key, so anyone could have taken them from the sewing studio—innocently—then, like ink pens, they could have been passed around from person to person, place to place, and ended up who-knows-where.

A wave of calm washed over me, then a surge of strength. I hadn't done anything wrong. There was no reason to act as if I had—and no reason to fear being questioned by Sheriff Grumman.

I headed down Dove Drive toward Main Street, my chin up, my steps lively. Still, a part of me was troubled. Rayna's words echoed in my head. She and Eleanor had argued. Rayna had become so enraged with her aunt over the issue of the increased rent that she'd yelled at her. Not a good way to have spent what turned out to be their last moments together.

I'd gotten the feeling that something deeper had been going on between Rayna and Eleanor. They were family so it wasn't unusual. But the situation with the rent increase, a situation involving money, took it to another level. I wondered if another issue had gone on between Rayna and Eleanor, something Rayna didn't want to admit to.

Rayna had told me she'd gotten so mad at Eleanor she *couldn't see straight*. Just how mad was that? Mad enough to follow her to the visitor center and murder her?

One thing I was sure about—Sheriff Grumman had told Rayna that Eleanor had been murdered. The deputies knew, the crime-scene techs knew, the mayor knew, which meant the entire town would know very quickly.

Would everyone know I was a suspect? Would they believe it? Everyone knew me, everyone would think the best of me. Right? Surely, they would.

It didn't help that the murder weapon was engraved with my name.

"Those shears . . ." I mumbled.

I'd been through the gossip, the talk, the remarks once already, when the shears had been donated to the sewing studio. Where else could a generous, thoughtful gift cause so much controversy, except in a small town?

When I got back to the bakery, Aunt Sarah was chatting with a customer at the display case. It took me a few seconds to recognize her. Peri Oliver, close to thirty, had short, brown, sensible hair and equally sensible clothes and shoes. She worked part-time at Barry's Pet Emporium and at an animal rescue.

"Hi, Peri," I said, as I walked past. "I haven't seen you in a while. How's it going?"

"Really good," she replied, with a big smile.

I'd never seen Peri in a bad mood, not even a sort-of bad mood.

Aunt Sarah passed her a small bakery box. "Sorry. But if something changes, I'll keep you in mind."

"That's all I ask. Thanks!"

Peri gave me a cheerful smile and left the bakery.

Aunt Sarah shook her head. "She's looking for work. She's hardly getting any hours at the pet store."

I knew Caitlin's dad was stingy with part-time help. He expected Caitlin to work in the store almost constantly since she was destined to carry on the business he'd spent decades building.

Aunt Sarah headed into the kitchen, checked her order book, and started pulling ingredients off the shelves. I followed and stood on the other side of the big work island. I had to tell her what was going on with Eleanor's death; letting my aunt find out the sheriff considered me a murder suspect wasn't something I was anxious to do. Still, I didn't want her to be the last to learn that Sheriff Grumman had me in his sights.

"How's Rayna?" Aunt Sarah asked.

"Upset. Bad enough to lose her aunt, but they'd argued the last time they were together," I said. "Over Rayna's rent, of all things. It had gone up."

"Hers too?" Aunt Sarah shook her head. "What a shame."

"Eleanor was murdered," I said.

She froze. "Murdered? I thought she had a heart attack."

"It gets worse. She was stabbed with shears."

Color drained from her face. "Not the ones . . ."

"Yes, the ones engraved with my name. The ones Gloria donated."

Aunt Sarah looked at me in the way that took me back to my childhood summers with her. Loving, kind, and without judgment.

"That doesn't mean you're involved," Aunt Sarah insisted. "Sheriff Grumman couldn't possibly think—"

"I'm sure he does," I said.

"But—"

The bell chimed as the front door opened. Sheriff Grumman walked into the bakery. He was in uniform, a no-nonsense shade of gray. While his deputies wore baseball-style caps, the sheriff's hat was wide brimmed. He headed straight for me, a grim expression on his face. Aunt Sarah circled the work island and stood beside me.

"Abbey just told me what happened to Eleanor," she said. "Surely, you don't think she had something to do with it."

"That's why I'm here." The sheriff turned to me. "You want to tell me what happened?"

His tone wasn't as accusatory as I'd expected. Still, I mentally clung to the fact that I was totally innocent, and the sheriff had no proof otherwise.

"I went to the visitor center to report for work," I explained. "Paige, then Kendall arrived shortly after I got there. We started sorting through the clothing for Lost and Found Day, and I discovered Eleanor's body in one of the bins."

Sheriff Grumman studied me for a long moment. "That's it? That's all that happened."

"That's it."

He was quiet for another few seconds, then said, "That's not what I heard."

My heart rate picked up a bit and my mind raced. These were the facts, the same facts I'd told Deputy Humphrey when he'd arrived.

"I have a witness who tells a different story." Sheriff Grumman leaned a little closer. His voice took on a harsh tone. "You were seen drenched in blood, hiding in the bathroom."

Now my heart rate doubled. Beside me, I felt Aunt Sarah tense.

"Blood? No—" Then I remembered my exchange with Paige. Harriet had mentioned the sheriff had already interviewed Paige. That's where he must have heard her version of events.

I heaved a sigh of relief. "It was tomato juice. The top popped off my travel cup and spilled all over my hand. I was in the bathroom washing it off when Paige came in."

"Tomato juice?"

"Yes, I brought it with me when I left the house."

"Can anybody confirm your story?" The sheriff must have seen the blank look on my face. "Maybe your aunt? Did she see you fill that travel cup with juice?"

Aunt Sarah had been at the bakery when I'd left the house.

I started to feel kind of queasy.

"Did you talk to somebody on the way to the visitor center?" he asked.

"Brooke," I remembered. "I chatted with her for a few minutes."

"Anybody else?"

I thought for a second. "No one else."

Sheriff Grumman nodded slowly. "We can put an end to this right now. Show me the travel cup. Prove to me it had tomato juice in it."

"Sure—"

The queasy feeling in my stomach turned icy.

He leaned a little closer. "You do have this supposed travel cup, don't you?"

"Well . . ." I gulped hard. I felt Aunt Sarah's worried gaze on my cheek.

"Well . . . what?" Sheriff Grumman demanded.

"I don't have it," I admitted.

"That's convenient," the sheriff smirked.

"It was gross. I didn't want it, so I threw it away."

"Even more convenient."

"I threw it in the Dumpster behind the visitor center. It's there. You can get it and see for yourself."

"We already checked the Dumpsters. They're all empty."

Aunt Sarah gasped. I did, too, remembering that I'd seen the trash truck in the parking lot just before I entered the visitor center.

"By your own admission, you destroyed evidence," Sheriff Grumman said. "You were the first to arrive at the visitor center, which means you were alone with the victim. I've got a witness who states you were washing off blood, and I've got a murder weapon with your name on it. You see how that looks?"

I didn't say anything—I couldn't get any words out.

"Ed, that's all very circumstantial," Aunt Sarah insisted. "It proves nothing."

Sheriff Grumman ignored her and stared at me, as if expecting me to confess.

"It looks to me as if I've found Eleanor's murderer," he said.

I pulled together every shred of courage I could muster and said, "All you need now is some evidence."

He glared at me for another few seconds. "And I'll find it."

Sheriff Grumman gave me a curt nod and left the bakery.

"He won't find anything," Aunt Sarah insisted. "He knows there's nothing to find. He'll move on. He'll let it go, don't you think?"

"No."

I believed what he said. He was convinced I'd killed Eleanor. I doubted he'd look any further.

That meant I was going to have to find her murderer myself.

CHAPTER 5

Had I missed Eleanor's killer by only a few minutes?

Since being questioned by Sheriff Grumman yesterday, that thought had run through my head the rest of the day, last night, and now this morning—I think I might have even dreamed about it.

As I headed down Hummingbird Lane, the vision of the crime scene in the visitor center's storage room continued to play over and over in my thoughts, like a bad movie on a continuous loop. Was something there, something obvious, something subtle that I'd seen yesterday when I'd found Eleanor's body, but hadn't realized was significant?

It was very possible, considering I hadn't realized shears with my name on them had been impaled in Eleanor's chest.

Main Street looked as peaceful and charming as always when I turned the corner and headed toward the visitor center. I wasn't on the schedule to work today, but I wanted to stop by and see if Harriet needed anything.

Nobody else I saw strolling Main Street seemed to be consumed with thoughts of murder. Lucky them. I also doubted anyone was consumed by thoughts of Deputy Zack McKenna, as I was.

I hadn't seen or heard from Zack since yesterday when he'd come to the sewing studio asking about shears and my possible involvement in Eleanor's murder. Even though I understood he was giving me a heads-up, I'd been hurt. I thought he'd come back and explain himself, but he hadn't. Still, my gaze swept the street looking for him.

I gave myself a mental shake and decided I'd rather think about the crime scene.

When I'd gotten to the visitor center yesterday morning, juggling my tote bag and travel cup, I'd been fixated on unlocking the door and wondering why Eleanor wasn't already there—the first to arrive, as usual. I remembered glancing around hoping to see her. I'd noticed nothing suspicious— no one running away, no one darting between the parked cars, no vehicle speeding out of the lot.

Rayna had told me Eleanor had been at her house that morning and, presumably, had then gone straight to the visitor center—which meant that if I'd arrived a few minutes sooner, or had been paying better attention, I'd likely have seen the murderer. Or, maybe, my presence there would have prevented the murder and Eleanor would be alive.

Not a great feeling.

I could have gotten there in time to stop the murder, or at least see the murderer, I realized, if Brooke hadn't stopped me to chat.

Another reason not to like her.

Across Main Street I saw Peri outside Barry's Pet Emporium. She placed the sign featuring the day's specials by the door and filled the bowls with fresh water. Good to see Caitlin's dad had scheduled her some hours today.

When I'd gotten inside the storage room yesterday, I hadn't noticed anything unusual, just the normal clutter. No sign of

a struggle, nothing to indicate there'd been a problem—
certainly not a murder. Paige, then Kendall, had arrived
moments after me. I wondered now if they'd noticed anything amiss.

Eleanor had likely been caught by surprise by the attack, I
figured. She probably knew her killer, thought nothing of it
when that person walked into the storage room.

My conversation with Rayna drifted through my thoughts
again. They'd argued. Rayna had been so mad at her aunt
that she'd yelled at her. Had Rayna, still furious, followed
Eleanor to the visitor center? Did Eleanor see her and think
she'd come there to apologize? Did Rayna, her anger out of
control, confront her, then kill her?

If that were true, Rayna would have a lot more to worry
about than the increase in her rent. Was that the real reason
she'd seemed so devastated when I'd been at her home yesterday?

My head started to throb, so I gave myself another mental
shake and picked up my pace.

Flights of Flowers was doing a brisk business, I noticed as
I passed the shop. Through their window I spotted Lily
straightening a display of green plants. Lily was about my
age, petite, and usually wore her blond hair in a ponytail. She
was a regular volunteer at my pillowcase dress parties. She
saw me and, instead of the little wave I expected, she held up
her hand as if wanting me to stop, just as a customer confronted her, pointing to something at the back of the shop. I
waved and kept going.

At the visitor center, the OPEN sign hung on the door. Inside I saw Harriet at the front counter flipping the pages of
one of the ledgers. She looked up when the little bell chimed,
and I walked inside. No one else was there.

"Are you on the schedule today?" she asked, frowning.

One of the many things Harriet worried about was payroll. The visitor center's budget was small and expenses had to be kept to a minimum, or so she told us nearly every day.

"I wanted to see how things are going." I looked around. "Isn't Paige working today? She's on the schedule."

Harriet grimaced. "I called. She's still hysterical. I'm worried."

Probably worried about a lawsuit, not that I blamed her.

"I called Kendall, asking her to come in," Harriet said. "I got her voicemail. She hasn't returned my call."

"Do you want me to work?" I offered.

"Things are quiet. I can handle it." She drew a heavy breath and let it out slowly. "I'm afraid we might have to postpone Lost and Found Day. I don't think anyone would want to go into the storage room to sort and price the items after what happened there."

I couldn't have agreed more.

"And all the clothing that was in the bin with . . . with Eleanor is at the crime lab," Harriet said. "I can't imagine people would actually buy something if we had the event, knowing . . . what happened."

"Have you heard anything about the investigation?" I asked.

"The sheriff wants to know if anything was stolen." Harriet gestured to the cabinets along the back wall where the found items deemed to be of value were kept, then held up the ledger she'd been studying. "I'm trying to decipher Gloria's records."

Gloria kept track of the lost and found luxury items turned in to the visitor center. She insisted that she—and only she—would handle the valuable designer merchandise, as if she was doing the rest of us a favor by taking on that responsibility. I guess she meant well, but her attitude had offended everyone who worked or volunteered at the visitor center.

"Gloria called and insisted on coming down after I mentioned the sheriff wanted me to check the luxury items inventory," Harriet said.

Gloria, apparently, wasn't uncomfortable coming to the visitor center. Hopefully, Kendall would feel the same and report for her shift.

"I told Gloria it wasn't necessary. I told her I could handle it," Harriet said. "But she's on her way."

Gloria was in the visitor center yesterday. She'd have noticed if the cabinet had been broken into.

The luxe cabinet, as Gloria called it, remained locked at all times, as if she suspected the rest of us would steal something; another way Gloria had managed to offend everyone. She had the only key. Harriet seemed okay with it; one less thing for her to worry about, I guessed.

"Honestly, it seems like a waste of time," Harriet said. "A theft. Really, I don't know what Sheriff Grumman is thinking."

I circled around the front counter and took a closer look at the cabinets. They were built-ins, probably decades old, made of what looked like particleboard. The door of the luxe cabinet, the only one ever locked, showed no sign of damage. There was nothing to indicate it had been pried open. I tugged on the handle. It didn't budge, but I doubted it would take more than a paper clip and a YouTube video to pop the lock.

"Would you like me to handle it?" I offered.

"Abbey, you're so sweet. I really appreciate it. You're always here to do more than your share," Harriet said, and smiled for the first time. "I tell everyone how fortunate we are that you're working here now."

The bell over the door chimed and Harriet and I turned, both expecting to see Gloria arrive. Instead, it was Janine.

Janine was mid-forties, with dark hair cut in a bob, and wore a self-imposed uniform of a butterscotch blazer and a beret. She'd run the visitor center before the town council hired Harriet. Some people had suspected Janine would be upset about being replaced, but she seemed okay with the change.

"Hello, hello!" Janine called.

Janine was super friendly.

"Hello, my dears, hello!" she said.

Janine got on my nerves.

She paused and her smile grew. "It's a beautiful day in our beautiful town!"

See?

Harriet didn't seem to know what to say to Janine, and I wasn't interested in trying, but Harriet made an attempt.

"We're all still reeling from Eleanor's death," she said.

"Sad. Sad, sad, sad." Janine frowned for a moment, then broke into a big smile. "Looks as if we need a morale booster!"

Neither Harriet nor I said anything.

"I have a fabulous idea!" Janine said.

The bell chimed again, and Gloria Marsh came into the visitor center, saving us from Janine's morale-boosting thought.

"I'm here. Don't worry about a thing," Gloria announced as she breezed across the room.

Gloria was in her sixties, I guessed. Her brown hair, which she'd recently dyed, was perfectly styled, and her nails were professionally manicured. The pantsuit she wore looked new and expensive. She carried a handbag that I recognized from my days working in Los Angeles, a designer brand that cost hundreds. She'd definitely upgraded her look lately.

"I thought I was going to have to ask Abbey to do the inventory for the sheriff," Harriet said.

Gloria paused in front of the counter and smiled sweetly.

"The luxe items are my responsibility. I handle them," she said, as if reminding a small child of the rules. "Remember, all you have to do is call. I can be here at a moment's notice."

Gloria's *moment's notice* was certainly longer than a moment, I thought. Harriet seemed to feel the same, but apparently, she didn't want to get into it with Gloria. Keeping volunteers, like Gloria, who were willing to donate their time to the visitor center was another aspect of Harriet's job that caused her some stress.

"I'll have this done in a jiffy." Gloria pulled the ledger out of Harriet's hands and headed for the cabinets.

"Now, about my morale booster," Janine said. "I have the most fabulous idea!"

"Sorry," I said, though I really wasn't. "I have to go."

"I'll fill you in later," Janine promised.

"Let me know if there's anything I can do to help," I said to Harriet, and hurried out of the visitor center.

I'd come here this morning with the intention of helping out, if I could, but I found myself walking away more concerned than when I'd arrived.

Paige was too distraught to report to work. Kendall hadn't returned Harriet's call. Lost and Found Day might cancel. How would the visitor center continue to serve Hideaway Grove if employees and volunteers wouldn't come in, and everybody avoided going into the storage room?

How much worse would it get when the whole town learned that Eleanor had been murdered?

The notion that my job could disappear if the visitor center closed hit me hard. Sure, the duties of the center would likely be transferred to another department, but there was no guarantee I'd be included. What would I do then?

Since I'd moved to Hideaway Grove, I'd been at loose ends, job-wise. I'd managed to generate a little income with my tote bag business, but mostly I'd been living off my savings. How would I make my car payment? How could I expand my business? Aunt Sarah had always said I didn't have to pay rent, but I'd left cash on the kitchen table for her every week. I couldn't expect her to let me live with her indefinitely, without offering her a cent. What would I do?

Small consolation that I wasn't in this alone, I thought. I couldn't bring myself to contact Paige, still upset, according to Harriet, so I stopped in front of the Eagle Art Gallery, pulled my phone from my tote, and called Kendall. Her voicemail picked up. I left a message.

I drew a determined breath, refusing to be discouraged. As I'd thought earlier, finding Eleanor's killer was the best way to avoid all my problems. I started walking with renewed commitment. All I needed were some clues, some evidence, a motive, and, of course, a suspect.

Thoughts of finding a murderer flew out of my head when, ahead of me on the sidewalk, Zack stepped out of the alley.

He centered himself on the sidewalk, blocking my path, forcing me to stop.

CHAPTER 6

Zack was in uniform, and he was looking directly at me.

My heart did its usual little pitter-pat, then my brain took over.

Our last encounter in the sewing studio when he'd confronted me about the shears used to murder Eleanor had been unexpected and upsetting. I didn't want to go through that again.

"Can you talk for a minute?" he asked.

He was tall with wide shoulders that looked even more impressive when he wore his uniform. He smelled great.

I didn't want him to look or smell great.

I steeled my feelings. "Is this an official interrogation?"

"No."

His gaze was intense as if something more than a conversation was on his mind. I wasn't sure what it was.

"What do you want to talk about?" I asked.

Zack paused, as if carrying on a mental debate.

"You hung around the visitor center yesterday, not wanting to leave," he said. "You kept volunteering to stay. Why?"

A few seconds passed before Harriet's kind words to me a few minutes ago came back, and I understood what he was getting at.

"You think—"

"—the sheriff thinks—"

"—I deliberately stayed there. Like it was some calculated plan on my part? To keep an eye on the investigation? To destroy evidence?"

"Did you?"

"No!"

"You shouldn't have lied," Zack said.

He kept his words calm and measured, as he'd been trained to do. Was there a tone of concern beneath them? Or was that wishful thinking on my part?

"Lied?" I shook my head. "I didn't lie about anything. What are you talking about?"

"That travel cup, the one you claim had tomato juice in it, the one you were seen in the bathroom with," he said. "A witness said it was actually blood."

"It was tomato juice," I insisted.

Zack hesitated a few seconds. "Another witness—"

"Who?"

"Another witness said you told her it was mineral water," Zack said.

"Mineral water?" I shook my head, confused. Then it hit me. I'd run into Brooke on the way to the visitor center and I hadn't wanted to tell her I was drinking juice because my favorite jeans were too tight.

No way was I talking about that now, especially to Zack.

"Okay, you got me. I lied about what was in the travel cup," I said, my anger growing. "What else have you got? How about some evidence? How about a motive?"

Zack opened his mouth to speak, but I plowed ahead.

"How about a little trust? Maybe a little faith?" I demanded. "Do you think I'd be here talking to you like this if I didn't believe you were innocent?"

Zack raised his voice, as I'd seldom heard him do before, as I'm sure he never allowed himself to do while in uniform, or maybe ever.

We stared at each other, tension high between us.

"Honestly," I said. "I'm not sure what to think."

I cut around him and walked away.

Ahead of me on Main Street I saw Geraldine come out of Sassy Fashions and march next door to the bakery. Today she had on a pink and yellow pastel dress; her expression looked anything but pleasant.

I knew what that meant. Just what I needed, after dealing with Zack.

I braced myself and went into the bakery.

Aunt Sarah stood behind the display case facing Geraldine on the other side. Anna was also there, along with Valerie, the owner of the Owl's Nest bookstore. No customers, thankfully; I was pretty sure I knew where their conversation was going.

"A bridal show," Geraldine exclaimed. "We've got a bridal show booked and now *this*."

"A murder." Valerie whispered the words, as if that might lessen their impact.

The news had broken about the true nature of Eleanor's death. I wondered if word had circulated that the murder weapon was personalized with my name.

"And the dish ladies will be here soon," Geraldine said. "What are they going to think? Are they going to cancel, too?"

Anna glanced at Aunt Sarah. "Is that sugar cookies I smell?"

Aunt Sarah ducked back into the kitchen.

"Poor Eleanor," Anna said.

"Poor Eleanor?" Geraldine exclaimed. "What about the rest of us?"

Everyone looked at her sharply and Geraldine shifted uncomfortably.

"What I mean is that here we are, once again worried about our financial future because major events might cancel," Geraldine said.

"It's like living in a house of cards," Anna said.

Aunt Sarah placed a tray of warm sugar cookies atop the display case. Anna took two.

"Something needs to be done," Geraldine declared.

"Like what?" Valerie asked.

Geraldine stewed for a moment, her lips pursed, her eyes narrowed.

"*Something*," she finally said.

"I've stocked every book I can find on brides and weddings," Valerie said. "And dishes, too. What am I going to do with them if both of those events fall through?"

"I've got bridesmaid's dresses stuffed to the rafters in my stockroom, ready to go for the bridal show. I ordered an expensive china pattern for my display window to go along with my wedding theme that I'm also using for the dish ladies. How am I going to get rid of all that inventory?" Geraldine said. "This could be a financial disaster."

"Times are hard." Anna helped herself to another cookie. "Rents are going up all over town."

"A rent increase? Here? In Hideaway Grove?" Valerie shook her head. "What kind of landlord would raise the rent? There's nothing in town to justify an increase."

"I don't understand why Eleanor—or anyone—would be killed in the visitor center," Geraldine said.

"I heard it was a break-in," Anna said around a mouthful of cookie.

"That's what I heard," Valerie agreed.

"To steal *what*?" Geraldine demanded. "There's nothing of value in the place. Is there?"

Everyone turned to me.

"Office equipment. The things the town uses for events and the holiday decorations," I said. "Some of the found items are designer. Really nice things."

"Used." Geraldine turned up her nose. "Who'd steal a *used* wallet or handbag or whatever?"

"That designer stuff holds its value," Anna reported, reaching for another cookie. "I see it all the time on eBay."

Gloria kept track of the luxury items, so I wasn't sure what was there, or what condition it was in.

"If it wasn't an attempt to steal something," Geraldine said, "why on earth would someone break in?"

Good question, I thought. The killer must have had a different plan. Was he looking for someone else, expecting to find not Eleanor at the visitor center, but another person? I remembered that Paige, Kendall, and I had all known Gloria was supposed to be there that morning. Was she the intended victim?

A creepy feeling came over me. If not Gloria, was it one of us?

"Sheriff Grumman better figure this out soon," Geraldine said. "We can't risk losing these two events."

"Is he making any progress?" Valerie asked. "Does he have a suspect?"

I held my breath, waiting to hear her answer. Aunt Sarah caught my gaze; I could tell she was worried about the same thing.

"He's not said a word," Geraldine said.

I heard Aunt Sarah's gentle sigh of relief.

"I called the sheriff's office," Anna reported. "Just the usual *it's ongoing* and *we're investigating*."

"I don't like this. I don't like this one bit." Geraldine's

eyes narrowed. "I don't like being put in this situation. Something must be done—it must."

With that, Geraldine left the bakery.

"I agree. We need to figure out a better way," Valerie said, and followed Geraldine out the door.

Anna pulled a small wallet from her pants pocket, fished out a few bills, and laid them on the display case. She grabbed three more cookies.

"I'll have pillowcases for you soon," she said to me, and nodded toward the sewing studio. "Hopefully, they won't be uglies."

The volunteers had dubbed the plain pillowcases *uglies*. We prettied them up with lace, rickrack, or other embellishments and transformed them into something the girls who received them would like.

"Thanks," I said.

Anna waved as she went out the door.

Aunt Sarah and I shared a look of relief that my supposed involvement in Eleanor's death wasn't making the rounds through town. If only it would stay that way.

I noticed then that Jodi wasn't at the bakery, and asked Aunt Sarah about her absence.

"Jodi was scheduled to work today. Something came up," she reported.

"Wasn't she supposed to help with the ideas for the bridal show?"

"That, and the dish ladies."

Aunt Sarah always prepared desserts for special events in Hideaway Grove. She baked for their meeting, plus featured specialty items in her bakery for attendees as they made the rounds through town.

"Do you need help?" I asked.

"I've got it under control, so far."

I went into the sewing studio, thinking about the pillowcases Anna donated. True, some of them were uglies, but I knew the volunteers were up to the challenge of transforming them. Anna's cousin in Los Angeles frequented estate sales and often passed along some truly exceptional pillowcases; hopefully, we'd get some of those, too. I checked the cardboard box under the cutting table where I stored the donated pillowcases. The box was almost full, which surprised me. I didn't realize I'd accumulated so many.

With all the thoughts of murder in my head this morning, I decided I needed to liven up my day. At the big windows that faced Main Street, I tugged on the shades a few times and finally got them to roll up.

Outside, shoppers strolled past the stores and cars drove sedately along the street. Off to my right, across the street in front of the drugstore, I spotted Deputy Humphrey. Owen looked handsome in his uniform, patrolling the area. Another lovely day in Hideaway Grove.

Feeling optimistic, I grasped the handholds of one of the windows and tried to lift it. It didn't budge. I yanked harder but still no luck. I tried the other window with no better results. Occasionally, I'd been able to open one of them. Now, it seemed, they were both hopelessly stuck.

I moved on to something I could accomplish.

Aside from the traditional sewing machines set up for the volunteers to use, I had an embroidery machine on another table. It was the key to the business I'd started.

Something else that had seemed like a good idea at the time.

I'd designed a cute little owl, Hideaway Grove's mascot, and paired it with clever phrases, and embroidered them on tote bags. I'd sold them at some of the town's festivals and at a few of the local shops.

I still thought it was a good idea, even though it hadn't turned out as well as I'd envisioned.

While I'd been fortunate to make contact with a woman who owned a chain of gift shops and who loved my bags, I'd quickly realized there was no way I could provide enough inventory for all of her stores. I was the sum total of my business—just me, making one tote bag at a time. I'd have to expand significantly, and I simply didn't have the funds for it. But she'd agreed to take a few bags each month, which I was grateful for, with the promise to take more when my production improved. That left me with nothing to do but keep going and hope for enough sales—and maybe a financial miracle—that could turn my idea into a profitable company.

I was about to grab a tote bag from my stock when urgent voices drifted in from the bakery. A few seconds later, Mitch Delaney strode into the sewing studio.

Mitch was a big guy, tall, broad shoulders, dark hair, handsome, and maybe around thirty years old. He'd been in Hideaway Grove a little longer than me, having left New York City for a quieter life, and now spent his days making internationally renowned custom furniture in his converted garage at his house on Hawk Avenue.

Worry drew his brows together and a light sheen of perspiration dotted his forehead. A sprinkling of sawdust covered his shirt, making me think he'd hurried here from his workshop, and sending a spike of alarm through me.

"What did Caitlin say?" he demanded. "Is she okay?"

Now I was more alarmed because I had no idea what he was talking about.

"I—what—"

"Haven't you heard?" Mitch asked, as if it was inconceivable that I hadn't. "Caitlin's dad had another heart attack last night."

CHAPTER 7

"What happened?" I demanded, my stress level spiking to match Mitch's.

"I was at the convenience store and the clerk mentioned it," Mitch said. "I don't know details. That's why I'm here. I figured you'd know."

It wasn't a secret that Caitlin and I were best friends. Nor was it a secret—at least to me, and no more so than at this moment—that Mitch was hopelessly in love with Caitlin.

"I'll call." I grabbed my phone and tapped her name in my contact list.

I felt like the worst friend on the planet because I suddenly remembered that yesterday she had said we should get together. I'd been so involved with Eleanor's murder that I'd forgotten all about it.

Caitlin's voicemail sounded in my ear. I left a message, then sent her a text asking about her dad and letting her know I was standing by if she needed anything. That wasn't enough, of course.

"Let's go over there," I said, gesturing out the window toward the pet shop across the street.

Mitch didn't move. He glanced out the window, then at me. I could see he was torn about what to do—for all the right reasons.

Caitlin was engaged. She'd been engaged for over a year, before Mitch had moved to Hideaway Grove. Mitch respected that, but it was hard for him, especially now when he wanted to go to her, help her, comfort her.

"Come with me," I said. "I'd rather not go by myself."

That seemed to be all the prompting Mitch needed. We hurried out of the sewing studio and into the bakery.

"Did you know Caitlin's dad had a heart attack last night?" I called to Aunt Sarah in the kitchen.

She looked up from the cupcakes she was icing, stunned. "No. Scott was just in here. He didn't mention it."

Scott Freedman was Caitlin's fiancé. He worked at the tire store his family owned out by the freeway entrance.

"We're going to the store," I said. "I'll let you know."

Mitch opened the door for me; we went out and dashed across Main Street. Peri stood at the pet store entrance refilling the water bowls. She looked slightly startled by our approach.

"What's going on with Caitlin's dad?" I asked.

Now Peri looked lost—and alarmed.

"I heard he had a heart attack last night," Mitch said.

"Well, that explains it," Peri said. "I got a text from Caitlin asking if I could open the store this morning. They never ask me to do that. I should have known something was wrong."

"She didn't mention her dad?" Mitch asked.

"No." Peri shook her head. "Why wouldn't she let me know? That's so strange."

It was more strange, I thought, that she hadn't let her fiancé know.

"What's going on with her dad?" Peri asked. "What's his condition?"

"We don't know. We're waiting to hear," I said.

"I'll text her and let her know everything is okay at the store. One less thing for her to worry about," Peri said, and headed inside.

Mitch and I looked at each other, both of us wanting to do something, but not knowing what it should be.

"Let's go back to the sewing studio," I finally said. "I should hear from Caitlin soon."

We crossed the street again and went into the bakery. Aunt Sarah was still swirling icing. I promised to update her when I heard from Caitlin.

In the sewing studio, Mitch paced and I shuffled pillowcases and sewing notions around, for something to do. I knew we were both worried, but I could see—and I understood—that Mitch's concern went deeper.

Mitch and I were alike on some level. Nothing romantic went on between us but we were connected. Both of us had lived in a big city—me in Los Angeles, Mitch in New York—with high-pressure jobs. Now we were adjusting to life in a small town and attempting to make a go of our own businesses.

The sewing studio grew warm, so I switched on the small table fan one of the volunteers had donated. Mitch strode across the room and grasped the handholds on one of the windows.

"They won't open," I said. "They're both stuck, that's why I use the—"

Mitch lifted. The window opened easily.

"—fan."

Men. They're so strong.

My phone buzzed. I yanked it out of the pocket of my jeans as Mitch crossed the room in three long strides.

"It's from Caitlin." I scanned her message. "She says her dad is okay. The doctor kept him at the hospital for several hours, ran some tests, then let him go home. She said she'll let me know more later today."

I felt some relief that Caitlin's dad was well enough to be sent home. Mitch looked more upset. I understood why.

"You want to be with her," I said.

We both knew that couldn't happen. Mitch couldn't impose himself on their family situation. It wasn't his place. He didn't belong there. She was engaged. He'd always respected her choice, but I could tell that for a while now, it was becoming more and more difficult for him.

"I'll let you know when I hear from her again," I promised.

Mitch nodded, then left the sewing studio.

I figured Caitlin and her mom were exhausted from being at the hospital with her dad during the night, so I texted her back letting her know I'd like to get together as soon as she was up to it and reminded her that I was here if she needed anything.

The sewing studio seemed suddenly empty. Faint voices drifted in from Main Street through the open window. I wandered around for a minute or two, then decided I may as well get some work done. A few orders for my tote bags had come in, and while it wasn't as many as I'd like, I needed to fill them promptly.

I checked the order on my phone and saw that the embroidery machine was already programed with the requested design and loaded with the correct thread colors. I grabbed a tote bag from my stack of inventory, slid it in place, and hit the button. The machine did the rest, stitching away, cutting the thread, changing colors so the design appeared as if by magic. It really was a sight to see.

But one bag at a time was slow. No way was I going to build an empire like this. I was going to have to figure out something else, somehow.

Chatter drifted in from the bakery. I recognized Caitlin's voice and a moment later, she walked into the sewing studio.

"Oh, my gosh, I've been so worried," I said, rushing to her. "How's your dad?"

"He's okay . . . considering."

She looked and sounded tired, yet her exhaustion seemed to run deeper than her worry about her dad and having spent most of the night at the hospital.

"The doctor said we got him to the hospital just in time," Caitlin said. "He's so stubborn. He didn't want to go."

"Men can be stubborn," I said. "But, given his previous health problem, this sounds foolish."

"He insisted Mom and I not let anybody know what was happening because he's afraid it might affect sales at the store. Can you believe it?" Caitlin said. "Then he was upset with me for staying at the hospital. He said I should go to the store. The store should be my priority."

"I was at the store earlier. Peri is handling it just fine."

"I know. She's very competent. I told Dad, but he wouldn't listen. He thinks his way is the only way."

"How's your mom?"

"Worried. Tired. She's with Dad now," Caitlin said. "We're expecting more test results from the doctor."

"Everybody's concerned," I said. "Aunt Sarah mentioned Scott was in the bakery earlier, but he didn't mention your dad."

Caitlin looked lost. "Scott?"

"Did you tell him what happened?"

"Oh." She nodded. "I suppose I should."

"You need to get some rest," I said. "I know you're exhausted."

"I am," she agreed. "I'm going to check on the store so I can let Dad know Peri has everything under control, then go home."

We left the sewing studio and crossed the bakery.

"Give your dad my best," Aunt Sarah called from the kitchen.

"I will," Caitlin replied.

"Let me know if you need anything," I said. "We're all here to help. Mitch stopped by. He's—"

"Mitch?" Caitlin stopped at the door, and I saw the only glimmer of relief on her face I'd witnessed today.

"He's worried, too," I said.

Emotions rose in Caitlin, but she gulped them down.

"Thanks," she murmured, and left the bakery.

I watched Caitlin cross Main Street and go into the pet store. I knew she trusted Peri to handle things, but I knew, too, that she felt obligated to do as her dad wished. I hoped she'd make it quick and go home for some rest.

I filled Aunt Sarah in on what Caitlin had told me about her dad's condition, sent a text message to Mitch with the latest, then went back into the sewing studio. I froze in the doorway. A gentle breeze flowed in through the open window and Cheddar sat on the sill. I couldn't help smiling as he gazed around the sewing studio, then looked at me.

"Nice to have company," I said.

Cheddar tilted his head one way, then the other, watching me.

"Can you stay awhile?" I asked, moving a little closer.

He meowed, then hopped outside, giving me my answer.

I hurried to the window, worried, afraid he might get hit by one of the cars on Main Street, but there was no sign of him. Somehow, he'd disappeared.

For a moment I envied Cheddar's freedom to come and go at will with no worries, no problems, no concerns.

"Abbey?"

I spun around and saw Lily hurry into the sewing studio. She looked frazzled and rushed. I figured she'd slipped away from the flower shop wanting to know if I'd heard about Caitlin's dad.

"Is it okay if I close the doors?" she asked, almost in a whisper.

Lily slid the pocket doors shut before I could answer, letting me know her visit wasn't likely about Caitlin's dad's health problems.

"What's up?" I asked.

She looked at the open window, then hurried to the other side of the room and motioned for me to join her.

"I'm worried," she said.

A jumble of ideas ran through my brain—events cancelling, the flower shop closing, losing her job, a killer on the loose. I braced myself.

Lily twisted her fingers together, grimaced, and gulped hard.

"I'm afraid ... I think ... well, something bad has happened," she said.

My worry doubled—what could be worse than all the thoughts I'd already had?

"Maybe," she added. "I don't know. I'm not sure."

I drew a breath to calm myself and said, "What's going on?"

Lily drew a calming breath, too, then leaned a little closer.

"I think Owen is cheating on my sister," she said.

My eyes flew open wide, and I gasped.

"What? No—but—" I stammered.

Deputy Owen Humphrey and Willow had been dating forever. They made a perfect couple. One glance at them together and it was obvious they were totally in love and destined to marry. They were the kind of couple everybody was happy for—and kind of jealous of.

"That's not possible," I finally said.

"I know. I thought so, too. Everybody thinks so," Lily said. "But lately Owen has been ... I don't know ... kind of distant. Secretive, sort of. He hasn't been spending time with Willow like always."

"You think that means he's cheating on her?" I asked.

"What else could it mean?" she asked. "You know how the two of them are."

I did. You seldom saw one of them without the other, except when Owen was on duty and Willow was working.

"Willow would lose her mind if she found out Owen was seeing someone else. She's crazy about him," Lily said.

"Does she suspect something's going on with him?"

Lily shook her head. "No, but I do."

"Did you see him with another woman?"

"I didn't. But two nights ago, Willow told me he cancelled their date. Said he had to work," Lily said. "Then I saw him driving out of town. Down that back road, the old way, before the freeway went in."

"Sneaking out of town," I realized. "Do you have any idea who he might be seeing? Someone who lives in Hideaway Grove?"

"I have no idea," Lily said. "I have to learn what he's doing. I can't let Willow find out first and be hurt. She'd die. She'd absolutely die."

"What are you going to do?" I asked. "Follow him? Spy on him? Try to catch him with someone else?"

"No," Lily said. "I want you to do it."

CHAPTER 8

Somehow, I was going to have to figure out who had murdered Eleanor—plus, find out if Owen Humphrey was cheating on Lily's sister. Lily had texted me a list of pertinent info on Owen—his home address, the license plate number of the black pickup truck he drove. Our plan was simple: she'd let me know when Owen broke another date with Willow, then I'd follow him, see where he went, see who he met. In the meantime, Lily wanted me to keep an eye on him, ask questions where possible, and find out as much as I could about what he was up to.

I've got no use for a cheater, so the idea that Owen might be doing just that really hit me hard.

Investigating Eleanor's murder seemed less upsetting.

I had little to go on, just my suspicion that Rayna had reached the end of her patience with her aunt, gone to the visitor center, and stabbed her with shears—shears that had my name on them. With no evidence and a motive that I'd made up in my head, I definitely had to come up with something substantial if I was going to solve this crime.

I decided to question Paige and Kendall. They were both at the visitor center when I'd found Eleanor's body. Maybe they'd seen or heard something I'd missed.

I left the bakery and headed for Dove Drive to the house where I knew Paige still lived with her parents. Paige wasn't my first choice to question—I knew I'd get more coherent information from Kendall—but I had to start somewhere. Plus, I figured I could get this over with quickly and move on.

Paige's family home was lovely, well kept, displaying the charm and storybook feel Hideaway Grove was known for. The house was painted lavender, trimmed in pink and a touch of yellow, with flowers in the front yard and a white picket fence.

At the front door I rang the bell and waited . . . and waited. No cars were parked at the curb or in the driveway, so I figured her parents were at work or running errands. I rang the bell again, waited some more, and was considering leaving when the door opened.

Paige peeked out. Her eyes were puffy and her nose was red, and she was wearing pajamas with unicorns on them. Behind her, the house was dark and silent.

"You're mad at me, aren't you?" she said, and tears popped into her eyes. "I don't blame you. But I had to tell the truth. I had to."

She was referring to the things she'd told Sheriff Grumman about the tomato juice she'd seen on me that she'd thought was blood.

"I'm not mad at you," I said, because, really, I wasn't. She'd told the truth as she saw it; there was nothing malicious about what she'd done. "I just came by to check on you, see how you're doing."

"Not very good," Paige said, and sniffed hard.

I thought that at this point she would invite me inside. She didn't.

Seemed this visit would be quicker than I'd imagined.

"Have you heard from Kendall?" I asked.

Paige shook her head. "No. I don't think Kendall likes me very much."

I couldn't disagree.

"But Harriet came by, and Gloria. They were both very nice. Especially Gloria. She was concerned that I might have seen . . . you know . . . something really awful in the storage room."

I hadn't expected to get to the reason I'd come here so easily, nor had I expected Gloria would have paved the way, but I went with it.

"What did you see, exactly?" I asked.

Paige thought for a few seconds. "Kendall. And you. You with all that blood on your hand."

I wished she'd stop saying that.

"When you got to the visitor center, did you see anybody else there?" I asked. "Outside? Maybe somebody leaving? Hurrying away?"

"Sheriff Grumman asked me that again."

"He came back?" I asked, a little alarmed.

Paige nodded. "All I saw was you and the blood."

Good grief.

"Tomato juice," I said. "I promise you, it was tomato juice."

"He asked me how you were acting when I saw you."

A wave of dread flowed through me.

"I told him how you were, you know, kind of hiding in the bathroom," Paige said. "That you wouldn't let me come in and help you. That you said nothing was wrong. That you made me leave, telling me to go fix coffee."

The wave of dread hardened into a knot in my stomach.

"Was it okay that I said that? I don't want to get you into trouble." Tears splashed onto Paige's cheeks. "I'm sorry if I got you in trouble."

I managed a weak smile. "It's okay, Paige. I'm not in trouble."

She wiped her tears with the backs of her hands. "I don't want to work at the visitor center anymore."

"You shouldn't," I agreed.

Paige nodded, then closed the door. I left.

So far in my investigation, I had one suspect with a flimsy motive and, well, nothing else—except the knowledge that Sheriff Grumman was still investigating *me*.

I pulled out my phone as I headed down Dove Drive and called Kendall. If anyone had something substantial to contribute, it would be her. Her voicemail picked up; I left a message. No way would I be deterred. I turned onto Main Street and headed for Kendall's house.

It seemed certain that Paige wouldn't return to work at the visitor center. We'd be short-staffed, with major events coming up. Even if Harriet cancelled Lost and Found Day, we'd be stretched thin handling the bridal show and the dish ladies. But would Harriet be able to hire Paige's replacement? Would anybody want to work there after Eleanor's murder? The possibility that the visitor center might shut down seemed more and more likely, leaving me without a job.

Not a great feeling.

Kendall lived with a couple of roommates on Hawk Avenue. As I turned the corner from Main Street I spotted Mitch pacing across his driveway, his phone at his ear, a frown on his face. His garage door was open. Inside the converted space were the tools and equipment he used to craft the custom furniture that had earned him a stellar, international reputation. I'd seen his work up close. Gorgeous beyond belief. His work surpassed *talented* to *gifted*.

I tried to catch his eye as I walked past, but he was intently involved with his phone conversation. I kept going.

The house where Kendall lived with friends looked like a typical rental—okay, but not great; I wondered if her rent was going up.

I rang the doorbell but didn't hear it echo inside the house. I knocked. The place had a deserted feel to it. No cars sat at the curb or in the driveway. I knocked again, gave it another minute or so, and walked away.

I wondered where Kendall was. Maybe out job-hunting. Maybe that's what I should be doing—as soon as I wasn't the sheriff's go-to suspect in Eleanor's murder.

When I reached Mitch's house, his garage door was closed, and his pickup truck was gone. I hoped that whatever his phone conversation had been about that had caused him to frown and pace was resolved.

My phone chimed as I turned onto Main Street. Hoping it was Kendall, I stopped and checked. It was a text from Harriet asking if I could work at the visitor center tomorrow; she hadn't heard from Kendall and didn't want to contact Paige. I wasn't on the schedule, but I was glad to do it—one more day of income. I sent her thumbs-up and smiley face emojis.

I headed down Main Street and, honestly, everybody I saw seemed to be having a better day than me. Peri stood outside the pet store chatting with customers while a tiny beagle sniffed her ankles; two ladies exited Sassy Fashions laughing and carrying shopping bags; a mom and a little boy headed into Dottie's Toys with huge smiles on their faces.

Mustering some inner strength, I drew a deep breath and reminded myself that things weren't that bad, I could handle them, and everything would be okay.

Then I spotted Deputy Owen Humphrey.

So much for my renewed effort.

Owen was in uniform, patrolling Main Street near the Nestlings Clothing Store, his gaze sweeping the area while nodding and speaking pleasantly to passersby. I'd always thought well of him, a big teddy bear of a guy, thoughtful, caring, committed to his work as a deputy sheriff and to his relationship with Willow. Now I saw him differently.

Willow and Owen had dated *forever* and obviously were totally right for each other. Even a casual observer could see their connection. When they were together, nothing else in the world seemed to exist for them. I'd always thought they were destined to be together always. Now I wasn't so sure.

Lily suspected he was involved with another woman. He'd cancelled a date with Willow and sneaked out of town. I didn't like a liar or a cheat. I didn't like to think Owen was guilty of those things. I hoped Lily was wrong.

This was a situation I had to be careful about investigating. I wasn't sure how I'd accomplish it, besides the plan Lily and I had come up with. Should I do more? Spy on him? Ask around town? He was a deputy. How would that look?

No matter what, I couldn't let Willow be blindsided, if he was being unfaithful. I'd figure out something.

Sarah's Sweets smelled knee-weakening delicious when I walked inside. Aunt Sarah stood behind the display counter chatting with several ladies—tourists, I guessed—as she boxed a dozen cupcakes for them. The women were weighed down with shopping bags, in high spirits, having a grand time— just what Hideaway Grove wanted for our visitors.

When they left, Aunt Sarah waved me into the kitchen.

"You're just in time. I need another opinion," she said.

Set out on the work island was an elegant teacup and

saucer with a yellow and pink floral design. The cup was filled and topped with toasted meringue.

"Wow . . ." I said.

"Lemon cake filled with raspberry sauce, topped with lemon curd, finished off with meringue." Aunt Sarah frowned and studied her creation. "What do you think?"

"It's beautiful," I said, slightly breathless. "I've never seen you make anything like it."

"First time I've tried it," Aunt Sarah admitted.

"Did you bake the cake inside the teacup?"

"Oven-proof. I found it at Anna's shop," she said. "It's for the dish ladies' luncheon."

"They will be blown away," I declared. "I sure am."

"I like the presentation." Aunt Sarah's frown deepened. "We need to do a taste test."

My struggle with the waistband of my favorite jeans popped into my head.

I glanced around the kitchen. "Where's Jodi? She's the best taste tester."

"Not working today," Aunt Sarah said. "I'll have her try it when she comes in again. For now, it's up to us."

Oh well, I decided. I'd just take a bite or two. It couldn't hurt. The battle of the waistband button hadn't been *that* bad.

Aunt Sarah dished out a generous portion of the cake onto two saucers and grabbed forks. I took a bite. The cake was still warm, and the raspberry filling and lemon curd complemented it perfectly. My eyes nearly watered.

"This is too good to be true," I managed to say.

Aunt Sarah chewed slowly, evaluating the taste and texture. Finally, she shook her head.

"I'm not so sure this is it," she said.

I took another bite, a small bite—really.

"Perfect," I declared. "The dish ladies will love it."

"Maybe a little more of the raspberry filling." Aunt Sarah suddenly looked tired. "I still have to figure out what to do for the bridal show. I want to do something totally different."

I eyed the last bit of cake remaining on my plate, every taste bud I had screaming for me to indulge myself. Somehow, I resisted.

"When's Jodi working again?" I asked.

Aunt Sarah and Jodi together created baking magic.

"I'm not sure," Aunt Sarah mumbled.

"I know she'll love this," I said. "You can always count on her to come up with great ideas for new things."

"That's true," Aunt Sarah said, still eyeing the dessert thoughtfully.

"Let me know if I can do something to help," I offered.

I rinsed our plates and forks, put them in the dishwasher, and headed for the sewing studio, leaving Aunt Sarah deep in thought.

When I slid back the pocket doors, I was surprised to see that I had a visitor. Cheddar lay under the cutting table, napping. He'd come in through the window again.

I rolled the doors closed. I didn't think Cheddar would venture into the bakery, but I couldn't take the chance. Aunt Sarah was fanatical about cleanliness, and rightly so.

Cheddar roused, arched his back, and yawned, stretching his jaws wide and sticking out his tiny pink tongue.

"Sleep good?" I asked.

He glanced at me, then wandered under the tables leisurely. At the rack that held the completed pillowcase dresses, he rubbed against the frame.

"I hope that means you approve of our designs," I said.

Cheddar gave me a ho-hum look, then dashed across the floor and leapt out the window.

I hurried over and peered outside. No horns blew, no brakes squealed. I guess Cheddar had once again made a safe getaway.

When I turned away from the window, I was surprised to see the pocket doors roll open and another visitor walk in, this one not so welcome.

Zack.

CHAPTER 9

Zack crossed the sewing studio. "Can we start over?"

I glared at him.

He wasn't in uniform; the khaki pants and blue polo shirt he wore softened his appearance. Still, I asked, "Is this official?"

A flash of something crossed his face—disappointment, maybe?—that I'd asked and that we both knew what it meant. Some of the trust between us was no longer there.

"No," he said.

True, he'd come to the sewing studio to give me a heads-up on Eleanor's murder and to warn me about the shears, and he'd stopped me on the street to share the latest in the investigation, even though it could have jeopardized his job or the sheriff's opinion of him. But he hadn't exactly been warm and compassionate. I'd gotten the feeling that, on some level, he'd wondered if I was involved.

The trust was gone. I wondered if the other feelings were gone, too.

Zack waved his hand between us. "This is just you and me. Talking."

He gave me a small smile, the one that curled up one side of his lips, the one that made my heart do a little flip-flop—usually. Not this time.

"What do you want to talk about?" I asked.

"You're investigating Eleanor's murder," he said, with a knowing look that was meant, I supposed, to remind me that we knew each other pretty well.

I didn't respond.

"So . . ." He drew a breath as if determined to press forward. "I thought we should exchange information."

This, I didn't expect. Law enforcement, especially in a small town like Hideaway Grove, kept details of a crime to themselves. But here he was, wanting to talk. I guess that showed he recognized the growing chasm between us and wanted to do something about it. I wasn't buying it, not completely.

"You first," I told him.

Zack studied me for a minute, mentally evaluating the situation, as he'd been trained to do, then flung out both arms and closed the distance between us in long strides.

"I'm sorry," he said, kind of loud, as if it were a release of emotions held in too long. "I messed up. I know that. I should have handled everything differently, right from the beginning. When I saw those shears with your name on them, I was scared—scared for you. I knew how it looked. I knew how the sheriff felt about you. I knew what you were in for, and I wanted to warn you, and I did it . . ."

"Badly?"

"Very badly."

"Thoughtlessly?"

"Thoughtlessly."

"Stupidly?"

"Stupid—well, hang on a minute."

Zack gave me a half smile and it made me melt a little. Just a little.

"So," he said. "Can we start over?"

Things between us still didn't seem right.

"Please," he whispered, with more sincerity than I'd ever heard from him.

Yes, things had changed, but being stubborn and unwilling to accept an honest apology and refusing to move on wouldn't make those things better again.

"Okay," I said, and managed a half grin of my own. "We'll start over."

Zack heaved an exaggerated sigh and his shoulders slumped, as if the weight of the world had been lifted. It was a little show for my benefit, but it made me smile.

"You want to talk about murder?" he asked.

"Doesn't everybody want to talk about murder when they're trying to improve a relationship?"

"We should work on that."

"Later."

"Right. Okay," he said, getting down to business. "What do you know about Eleanor's murder?"

"You first."

He grinned, seeming to enjoy the challenge I'd just thrown down.

Men. I swear.

Zack made a vague gesture toward Main Street. "Would you like to go somewhere and talk?"

Yes. I'd like to go *somewhere*. Somewhere away from Hideaway Grove, away from my business that wasn't going anywhere, away from Owen cheating on his girlfriend, away from Mitch pining away for Caitlin, away from the image of Eleanor impaled with shears, away from a murder investigation, away—from Zack? And if I did get away, then what?

"No," I said. "Let's talk here."

My decision didn't seem to suit him, but he went with it.

Zack pulled two chairs from the sewing tables and placed

them beside the rack of pillowcase dresses and the open window. He gestured grandly for me to sit. A gentle breeze flowed in bringing with it the murmur of voices and traffic. He sat down, adding his scent and the heat that always rolled off him, and scooted his chair a little closer than necessary to mine.

"We've made no progress in the investigation," he reported. "No clues, no motive, no security footage, no witnesses."

"I guess that means the only suspect is me," I said.

"Afraid so."

So far, nothing about this chat was making me feel any better.

Zack said, "Tell me about those scissors—"

"—shears."

"Whatever. How did they end up at a crime scene as a murder weapon?"

"I don't know," I told him.

Zack waved his hand toward the line of sewing machines behind us. "The shears, they're yours, right? They have your name on them. They must be special. You had them engraved."

"Oh, those shears!"

I said it kind of loud because I was sick to death of dealing with the shears—and not just since Eleanor had been murdered with them. They'd been nothing but a problem, caused nothing but unrest and dissent since I'd laid eyes on them. Even for gossip in a small town, it was too much.

"Tell me what happened," Zack said, in that calm, soothing way he had, the one that meant he was listening, and he could help.

I drew a breath forcing myself to rein in my emotions.

"First of all, you have to understand something," I said. "Lots of women volunteer for my pillowcase dress parties.

When I get enough pillowcases, I text my core group and let them know when the party is set for. They come, or they don't. Other times, women just show up. They heard about the charity, they want to help, so they come. Everybody is welcome."

"So far, I'm not hearing anything controversial."

"The women are generous with their time—and other things," I went on. "They stop by with donations. It's not unusual for me to walk in here and find a stack of pillowcases, or spools of thread, or lace, or rickrack. It just shows up."

"So, the scissors—"

"—shears."

"Whatever. They just appeared?"

"I wish."

I blew out a heavy breath attempting to keep myself calm, then continued.

"Eleanor came to a party and donated six pairs of scissors—"

"Shears."

"Scissors."

Zack shook his head, confused.

"They were scissors, not shears," I said. "I was glad to have them. The volunteers appreciated them. They were new, sharp, perfectly usable."

Zack studied me closely, as if waiting for me to get to the point.

"Inexpensive," I said.

He kept staring, still waiting for the reason for this whole story.

"Eleanor presented them to everyone, everybody oohed and aahed, they thanked her, I thanked her, and everybody was happy," I said.

He frowned, his confusion growing.

I pushed on. "A few days later, at the next pillowcase dress party, Gloria—"

"Gloria . . . ?"

"Gloria Marsh. She lives on Blue Bird Lane, she volunteers around town, her husband died recently."

"Right. I remember. He was a great guy."

"So, Gloria showed up with four pairs of shears. Expensive ones. Engraved with my name."

Zack's frown deepened, as if he was really attempting to understand—and didn't.

"Gloria's donation didn't go over well with most everyone," I explained. "It looked as if she'd bought the expensive shears and had them engraved just to upstage Eleanor's donation."

"And that upset people?" Zack seemed to understand but didn't *get it*. "Really?"

"Absolutely. Some of the volunteers thought it was a generous gift. Some thought Gloria had done it to spite Eleanor," I explained. "The talk, debate, the complaints went on for weeks. Every time I had a pillowcase party, every time somebody picked up a pair of shears, it came up again."

"Was it really about the scissors—shears?" Zack asked. "Or was something else going on? Did Gloria and Eleanor dislike each other?"

Something I'd noticed about women when they got into their late fifties and sixties, as Eleanor and Gloria were, they tended to be competitive. They also got cranky. I supposed it was from a lifetime of going along to get along, dealing with husbands, raising children, and everything else women had to put up with.

"I don't really know," I said.

"So people come by frequently? They come in here and drop off donations?" Zack asked.

"Exactly."

"If people are coming and going, wouldn't your aunt notice?" he asked.

"Maybe. Maybe not. She's busy baking, taking phone orders, waiting on customers," I said. "Even if she noticed someone going into the sewing studio, she wouldn't think anything of it."

"Anybody—the killer—could have come in and taken the shears," Zack concluded.

A ball of orange fluff popped up onto the windowsill in front of us.

"Back so soon?" I said.

Cheddar tilted his head, turned to Zack, laid back his ears and hissed, then disappeared out the window again.

"Did you train him to do that?" Zack asked.

"He's an excellent judge of character."

Zack got up and closed the window, then sat down again.

"Somehow, a pair of shears that were here in your sewing studio ended up in the hands of a killer," Zack said.

"And why would someone want to murder Eleanor? Eleanor, of all people? Everybody seemed to like her. She was active in charities, in civic matters and events. She cared about what was best for Hideaway Grove."

"Wrong place, wrong time?" Zack speculated.

I wondered, not for the first time, if I'd missed the murderer by moments. If so, Paige and Kendall had, too. And what about Gloria? If she hadn't come in late, she might have seen the killer.

"That would mean somebody broke into the visitor center, Eleanor confronted him, and he killed her." I shook my head. "But why would somebody attempt to rob the visitor center? There's nothing of value in there, except maybe the luxury found items."

"The what?"

"The expensive items tourists have lost that are turned in to the visitor center," I explained. "The *found* items."

"None of them were taken," he said.

"Where does that leave us?"

"The killer was there for a reason," Zack said. "Looking for *someone*, not *something*?"

"Such as, who?" I asked. "Maybe ... I don't know. Maybe Kendall?"

"Why her?"

"I don't know her well. We just met working at the visitor center. She hasn't lived in town for very long. She doesn't talk about herself much," I said. "I wondered if something—someone—from her past had come back to haunt her."

Zack was quiet, seemingly thinking over what I'd said.

"What did she tell the sheriff?" I asked.

"He hasn't questioned her yet," Zack said. "He's trying to contact her."

"So, if it wasn't a foiled robbery and the murderer had come to the visitor center with the intention of killing someone, who would have been the intended victim?" I wondered. "It could have been Paige, Gloria, Harriet, or Kendall."

"Or you."

CHAPTER 10

"It's always slow this time of day, isn't it," Harriet said.

I heard a note of desperation in her voice. I couldn't blame her for worrying.

We were in the visitor center. Harriet stood by the front counter. I sat at one of the desks. It had been quiet all morning. No tourists had come in, the phone hadn't rung. I wondered if out-of-towners had heard about Eleanor's murder in our storage room, were afraid and were staying away. I'm sure Harriet was thinking the same—and stressing about it.

"If Sheriff Grumman would get this . . . situation . . . resolved quickly, that would certainly help," Harriet said.

After what Zack told me in the sewing studio yesterday, that didn't seem likely to happen anytime soon.

"Have you heard from Kendall?" I asked.

"Not a peep."

Kendall, too upset to return to work, surprised me a little; another reminder that I didn't know her all that well.

"Unless I hear something from her soon, I'll have to replace her," Harriet said. "I don't know when Paige will come back."

Probably never, I thought. She'd told me as much yesterday. But I didn't mention it to Harriet. It wasn't my news to tell. Besides, Paige might change her mind and decide to return.

Harriet gasped. "You don't think . . . I mean, is it possible? The two of them are planning a lawsuit?"

Leave it to Harriet to stress about something that hadn't even happened, something she'd made up in her head.

"They would have included you," Harriet said, and glared at me, thinking, apparently, that I was now the enemy.

"I don't think you have anything to worry about," I said. "Paige is just rattled by Eleanor's death. Kendall too, probably."

"At least Gloria isn't afraid to be here," Harriet said, as if Gloria was the hero of the day. "She's not concerned that the killer might come back, thank goodness."

"You asked her?"

"She told me. She promised she wouldn't let me down."

"She's okay with handling the lost-and-found luxe items?" I asked.

"Yes, and good thing." Harriet gestured to the ledgers stacked atop the file cabinet. "I don't know how anyone else could figure out her tracking system."

I had a business degree. I was confident I could handle it. Plus, I was bored out of my mind.

Only Harriet was here, so I had no one to chat with except her, and today, as usual, she was too stressed to make small talk. She hadn't decided whether to cancel Lost and Found Day. If she decided to go ahead with it, at least I'd have something to fill my hours—not that I was all that anxious to go into the storage room to sort and price the items, with the vision of Eleanor's death fresh in my mind. Figuring out Gloria's inventory of lost-and-found luxe items would give me something to do.

"I can take over," I offered.

"No need. Gloria's willing and able," she said. "She's holding up so well since her husband died. So brave of her to carry on."

I drummed my fingers on the desk, wondering how any of us would be here to carry on if things didn't pick up.

The phone rang. I lunged for it, but Harriet got there first.

She sounded chipper, anxious to please, as she spoke to the caller. From her side of the conversation, I got the idea it was a travel agent interested in bringing a group of seniors to town for a day of shopping.

I rose from the desk and went to the front of the office. The local sightseeing brochures in the display rack by the door were in fine shape, but I decided to straighten them for something to do. I shuffled them around, squared them off. My mind drifted to yesterday when Zack had come to the sewing studio. Seeing him, being close to him, made my heart ache a little, especially since things didn't feel right between us.

Maybe it was because all we talked about was murder.

The front door swung open, jarring me from my thoughts. Brooke rushed inside, looking great in yoga togs, carrying a designer handbag, her makeup perfect, and not a hair out of place.

I was on my knees rearranging brochures.

She stopped short and beamed her ever-present fake smile at me.

"Just look at you, working," she said. "Isn't that the cutest thing?"

I hate her.

"Hello, Brooke," Harriet called, as she hung up the phone.

"Harriet! The most wonderful thing is happening!" Brooked scurried to the counter. "I know you can't wait to hear!"

The phone rang. I leapt to my feet, dashed to the desk farthest from the counter, and answered. I plastered my palm against my ear to block out Brooke's *wonderful thing*.

"Hideaway Grove visitor center," I said, and somehow managed to sound pleasant, rather than desperate for someone to talk to—who wasn't Brooke. "How can I help you?"

"Could I speak with Gloria, please?" a woman asked.

I pressed my palm harder against my ear.

"Sorry, she's not here right now. This is Abbey. Can I help you with something?"

"Oh, dear. I don't think so. I've been speaking with Gloria." The woman sounded elderly and upset, as if she was nearly at her wit's end.

Brooke's voice got louder. I circled the desk, stretching the curly phone cord to its max.

"Is this about a lost or found item?" I asked.

"My Burberry wallet. I lost it, somehow, when I was there for a day of shopping with my daughter and our friends. I don't know how it happened. I'm always careful with it," the woman said, sounding more and more distressed.

"Those are such nice wallets," I said. "I know it's upsetting for you."

I'd never owned anything by Burberry, but I knew their merchandise was beautiful—and crazy expensive. I felt bad for her—but mostly, I wanted to keep this conversation going until Brooke left.

"It was a gift, and very dear to me," the woman said. "This is the third time I've called. Gloria said she'd check and let me know if it was turned in, but I haven't heard from her."

This didn't seem like a good time to mention we were a bit behind on things because one of our volunteers had been murdered.

"I'll check," I said.

"Oh, thank you. That would be wonderful," she said. "My name is Lois. Lois Atwater."

"Hold on a minute, please."

I laid the receiver down and grabbed the luxe log off the top of the filing cabinet. At the front of the room, Brooke was still yammering on about whatever *thing* she considered *wonderful*.

I flipped the ledger open and gasped. Yikes! This thing was a mess. The list of lost-and-found luxury items, and the names of the people who'd reported them missing or recovered, was written in three different colors of ink—red, yellow, and green. Items were highlighted in orange and blue, and sometimes yellow. Lines were drawn up and down the pages, as if to connect certain items. Giant red arrows pointed to a few of the names. A large section had been completely covered with a pink colored pencil.

Harriet wasn't kidding when she'd said no one else could figure out Gloria's tracking system. But with Brooke still at the counter, still yakking, I was more than willing to try to solve Lois's problem.

I picked up the phone again.

"This will take a minute, Lois," I said. "Do you mind holding?"

"No, dear. I don't mind at all."

Once more, I laid the phone down and focused on the luxe log. I flipped pages back and forth, ran my finger down the column of names, followed the red lines that meandered from up and down, and finally I spotted Lois's name, highlighted in blue for no apparent reason. From there, I followed another red line to the bottom of the page and a large red arrow that seemed to indicate more info was on the previous page. There, I finally spotted a notation—written in yellow, who knows why—that Lois's Burberry wallet had been recovered and returned to her.

"Good news," I said to Lois when I picked up the phone. "Your wallet was recovered."

"Oh, dear. Oh, dear. Oh, thank goodness."

"And it was returned to you three days ago," I said.

"It was? Oh, how wonderful."

"It's on its way," I said. "You should have it shortly."

"Thank you. Thank you so much," she gushed.

Brooke seemed to have permanently stationed herself at the counter, so I tried to keep my conversation going with Lois.

"Did you enjoy your visit to Hideaway Grove?" I asked, then added quickly, "except for losing your wallet."

"I was there with friends, and my daughter, of course. She seldom takes time away from the office. We had a lovely day," Lois said. "Well, again, thank you for your help."

Lois, apparently, had something to do that was more fun than my prospect of dealing with Brooke. She thanked me again and we hung up.

"Abbey!" Brooke sang my name as if we hadn't seen each other in years.

If only.

Harriet made a break for the other side of the office, leaving me trapped at the desk facing Brooke at the counter.

"I'm so glad I caught you here . . . working," Brooke declared. "You remember that we're renewing our vows?"

I did. Unfortunately.

"I'm having a girls' night out—a bachelorette party! Ten of us out on the town, partying the night away."

I didn't say anything.

Brooke's usual fake smile morphed into a you're-going-to-love-this smile.

Did that mean I was invited to the party? Finally, Brooke was including me in something?

"So . . ." Brooke paused, letting the moment build. "I want you to make special tote bags for us!"

What had I been thinking?

"I know you're slow getting the bags done. Plus, you have to . . . work . . . now. So don't worry. I'll get the design and all the details to you soon."

Brooke didn't wait for my response, just flashed a big smile and hurried out of the visitor center.

I spent the rest of my four-hour shift trying not to think about things that were upsetting—Brooke's tote bags, Eleanor's murder, my failing business, whether I'd have a job here if things didn't pick up. I was totally unsuccessful. Those things were *all* I could think of. When I left, I decided to tackle my problems head-on. I started with finding Eleanor's killer.

I made my way down Main Street and turned onto Hawk Avenue. I expected to see Mitch's garage door open as he worked inside, but there was no sign of him.

When I got to Kendall's place, it looked as deserted and forlorn as the last time I was here. I was surprised to hear music bumping inside as I knocked on the door. A moment later, the door opened and a guy I'd never seen before looked out at me.

I figured him for early twenties, tall, dark hair sticking out, whiskers on his chin. He had on jeans, no shirt or shoes.

I knew Kendall had roommates, but, for some reason, this guy wasn't what I pictured.

He squinted at me. "Yeah?"

The room behind him was dark. An unpleasant smell wafted out around him.

"I'm looking for Kendall."

"Gone."

"Gone where?"

He shrugged. "Just gone. She took off. Packed her stuff and left."

This, I hadn't expected.

"When?" I asked.

He frowned, as if recalling something—anything—was a chore.

"I don't know. Yesterday, maybe? Couple of days ago? I don't know," he said. "Left me in a jam—rent's going up and she took off."

"Did she say where she was going?" I asked.

"She didn't say nothing." He waved toward the inside of the house. "You want to move in?"

"A forwarding address, maybe?"

"Nope. I could make you a good deal on the rent."

"If you hear from her, ask her to call me," I said, and told him my name.

"Sure," he said, but I doubted it would happen.

"Thanks," I said.

"If you change your mind about living here, let me know," he called as I walked away.

I headed down Hawk Avenue trying to sort out what I'd just learned.

Kendall had left town a day or so after Eleanor's murder. No notice, apparently, just grabbed her things and took off. Why?

Had she been afraid? Had she seen something that morning in the storage room that made her realize she knew the identity of Eleanor's murderer? Had she feared for her safety if she named the killer?

Or was something else going on?

I paused at the corner of Main Street, thinking, remembering.

That morning, when I was washing off the tomato juice in

the bathroom and trying to calm Paige, Kendall had seemed to suddenly appear. I hadn't seen or heard her come in. She was just there.

Maybe she'd been there all along.

A chill went through me at the thought.

Had Kendall murdered Eleanor, hidden amid the clutter of the storage room, and pretended to arrive after Paige and I got there?

It was possible, I realized.

But how would I prove it now that she'd left town?

CHAPTER 11

A glorious morning in Hideaway Grove greeted me as I left Aunt Sarah's house. A pleasant breeze, gentle sunshine, and the delightful fragrance of blooming flowers wrapped me in a cocoon of contentment—or would have if I could stop thinking about Eleanor's murder.

Most of the night I'd tossed and turned, my mental list of suspects continually rotating through my thoughts. Admittedly, I'd come up with only a few, and I'd discovered no evidence or clues. But, according to Zack, the sheriff hadn't uncovered even that much, so I didn't feel so bad.

Rayna topped my list. She was Eleanor's niece. They were family. Everybody knew what it was like with family; that alone could have made her my number one suspect. But more than that, she was the only person whom I'd found so far with a motive for killing Eleanor, thin though it was.

She'd described her aunt as a crusader, always championing some sort of cause, with a strong sense of right and wrong—which, apparently, she'd attempted to impose on Rayna. They'd argued about, of all things, a rent increase;

this, likely, wasn't the first thing they'd disagreed over. Rayna had been angry with her over the issue. Had she finally gotten so fed up with Eleanor's do-the-right-thing preaching that she'd decided to shut her up permanently?

Next up on my whodunit list was Kendall. I hadn't actually seen her arrive at the storage room that morning—she'd just appeared. I'd wondered if she'd been there all along, hiding, after stabbing Eleanor. With no motive or evidence, I knew including Kendall on my list was a stretch—or would have been if she hadn't left town suddenly without telling anyone. Definitely suspicious.

And Paige? She'd appeared out of nowhere that morning, it seemed. I tried to picture her attacking and stabbing Eleanor, but, thankfully, the image wouldn't form; I didn't need any more ugly pictures in my head. Paige struck me as too nervous, too young, too *everything* to murder someone. I couldn't see putting her on my mental suspect list.

How about Gloria? I wondered. She was supposed to be at the visitor center that morning. Was there a reason she hadn't arrived on time, as planned? Did she know something she wasn't telling?

Of everyone who worked and volunteered at the visitor center, Gloria was the only one, besides me, who wasn't worried about being there again. She had no concern that the killer might return. She'd come out and specifically told Harriet just that.

Gloria's husband had recently passed away. Maybe the possibility of dying didn't trouble her. Still, I kept her on my mental list. She was supposed to be at the visitor center, and she wasn't. Did it have something to do with Eleanor's death? I needed to find out.

I arrived at Sarah's Sweets no closer to figuring out who murdered Eleanor, but with a poor night's sleep and a slight headache.

"Good morning!" a voice called when I walked inside.

Aunt Sarah stood in the kitchen, the phone at her ear as she consulted the delivery schedule pinned to the wall. Jodi stood behind the display counter arranging a tray of muffins. She looked up and realized it was me who'd walked in.

"Abbey, you're just in time," she declared. "Cinnamon muffins, fresh out of the oven."

Jodi, thirtyish, with dark hair, huge blue eyes, and a curvy figure, added more to Sarah's Sweets than her baking talents. She had a way with customers—locals and tourists—that kept them coming back.

"Have one." Jodi gestured to the muffins.

My mouth actually watered, and my knees quivered slightly. They looked delicious. Cinnamon was one of my favorites. But thoughts of my struggle with my jeans' waistband intruded—even less welcome than Eleanor's murder.

"Maybe later," I said. "I haven't seen you in a while. Where have you been?"

"Wish I could say I was on a hot date with a good-looking man, but it was just some routine appointments," Jodi declared with a mischievous smile, then waved toward the sewing studio. "Speaking of which . . . you have a visitor."

A good-looking man ready to take me on a hot date?

Somehow, I didn't think it was Zack waiting for me—unless he wanted to talk about murder again. Not exactly my idea of a date, hot or otherwise.

I was pleasantly surprised when I walked into the sewing studio and found Mitch there. He stood in front of the windows, the shades rolled up, the windows wide open, his toolbox at his feet.

"I came by to fix your windows," he said. "I hope you don't mind."

Dressed in jeans, work boots, and a black T-shirt that

clung to his upper arms and chest, it was obvious the physical labor of making custom furniture was time well spent.

For a moment I envied Caitlin.

"Great. Thanks," I said.

Mitch gestured through the window to the pet store across the street. "Have you heard from Caitlin this morning?"

She, of course, was uppermost in his mind.

Again, I envied her.

I'd gotten a text message from her last night letting me know things were the same. I'd texted Mitch with the info. Caitlin hadn't responded to the texts I'd sent her earlier this morning.

"Nothing new since yesterday," I said.

He looked disappointed. "How's her dad?"

"Still waiting for test results, last I heard."

Mitch nodded and glanced out the window again, an unmistakable yearning creating a deep frown on his face.

"Looks like Peri is managing the store today," he noted.

I joined him near the windows. Across the street, Peri chatted with customers outside the store's entrance. I wondered how Caitlin's dad was handling the fact that she, apparently, wasn't running the store.

"Where is Caitlin?" Mitch murmured, mostly to himself.

His voice strained with worry—and a longing that made my heart ache for him. I wished I could make things better. All I could think to do at the moment was change the subject.

"I was by your house yesterday," I said. "You were heavily involved with a phone call."

My comment seemed to break the spell. Mitch knelt and rifled through his toolbox.

"A client," he said. "Wants me to take on another project for him. Big job."

"That's good news," I said, trying to put some enthusiasm into my voice. "Are you going to take it?"

"I haven't decided yet."

So much for changing the subject. I tried again.

"I stopped by to see Kendall," I went on. "Do you know her?"

Most everybody knew most everybody in Hideaway Grove. Mitch lived just a few doors down from Kendall's place.

He paused, thinking.

"She lives across the street from you, down at the end of the block," I added. "The blue house."

"The rental," he said. "Always a lot of people coming and going at that place. Some kind of trouble a few days ago. I saw the sheriff's car there."

Had I stumbled over a clue? Was this somehow related to Eleanor's murder?

"What kind of trouble?" I asked.

"I don't know. I got busy with a phone call. When I looked again, the sheriff was gone."

"I was there because I was concerned about Kendall," I said. "She was at the visitor center when Eleanor's body was found. She hasn't been back to work."

"Can't blame her," he said, still moving tools around. "Any progress on the investigation?"

"None," I said. "Anyway, Kendall left town. I wondered if maybe you had spoken with her, if you knew where she'd gone."

Mitch shook his head. "No."

Then I realized, good grief, here I was in the company of a hot-looking guy and, like with Zack, I was talking about murder.

Mitch stood, a tape measure in his hand. He glanced out the window and his face brightened.

"There's Caitlin—oh . . ." His shoulders slumped.

I gazed out the window and spotted Tristin Terry standing in front of Birdie's Gifts and Gadgets. Tristin was blond and resembled Caitlin. I'd mistaken her for Caitlin myself.

Tristin's family had lived in Hideaway Grove for years, then moved away when Tristin was in high school, or so I'd been told. They'd returned a short while ago. Caitlin had mentioned her, saying that she'd dated Caitlin's now-fiancé Scott back in the day. I'd intended to invite Tristin to my pillowcase dress parties but somehow hadn't done it yet. Something about Tristin troubled me, though I couldn't put my finger on exactly what it was.

Mitch, disheartened, unfurled the tape measure, then stopped short when Cheddar jumped up onto the windowsill.

"Hello again," I said.

Cheddar sat and curled his tail lazily.

"This cat gets around," Mitch commented.

Cheddar seemed to lighten the mood. He sat for another minute, then leapt from the window into the sewing studio. He meowed and wound between Mitch's ankles. I couldn't help but remember the decidedly different greeting Zack had gotten from Cheddar.

"He likes you," I said.

Cheddar circled another minute, then trotted to the pillowcase dress display rack. He rubbed against each of the legs. Seems he had definite opinions on men and pillowcase dresses.

"Fashion critic?" Mitch asked, grinning.

Cheddar returned to Mitch, headbutted his calf, then hopped over the windowsill and disappeared.

At the same moment, Mitch and I seemed to realize we had work to do. He started on the windows, and I got busy stitching tote bags. I had about a dozen more to do to fill the order I'd received from the gift shop chain. After that, the only thing on my financial horizon was the totes for Brooke's bachelorette party.

I needed the money, of course, but I wasn't all that anxious to get involved in a business deal with Brooke. She'd told me she would give me the design she wanted on the totes, and I mentally cringed thinking what it might look like. I'd dealt with designs provided by clients before and, often, they weren't done by professionals and were hideous.

I could only imagine what Brooke might come up with—her face, plus her entire life's story stitched into every square inch of the tote bag.

My phone buzzed, rescuing me from those awful thoughts, and I saw that I'd gotten a text message from Harriet. She required my presence at the visitor center immediately.

I hoped that didn't mean the dish ladies and the brides had cancelled.

I really hoped it didn't mean that somebody else had been murdered there.

"I've got to go," I said to Mitch, and held up my phone.

He nodded. "I've got to get back to the workroom. I need to check on something."

"Your client with the big order?"

Mitch nodded again, though he didn't seem happy about the prospect of a major project.

I gathered my things, and we left the sewing studio together. Mitch promised to come back later and continue repairs on the windows. Outside, he turned right toward Hawk Avenue. I went the other way toward the visitor center.

As usual, I found myself checking both sides of Main

Street, hoping to spot Zack. No sign of him, but I did see Gloria carrying a large shopping bag with several boxes peeking out, heading toward the post office. I wondered if she'd been summoned to Harriet's emergency meeting, too.

I held my breath as I passed Flights of Flowers, hoping Lily wouldn't see me—which was bad of me, of course. But I hadn't made any progress finding out what Owen was up to, if he was cheating on Lily's sister, and I didn't want to admit it—again, bad of me.

Hearing my name shouted over the hum of traffic on Main Street brought me up short. I whirled and spotted Caitlin, running, dodging cars, and waving frantically. My breath caught. I hurried toward her. She jumped onto the sidewalk in front of me.

Something awful had happened. Color had drained from her face. She gulped hard, trying to calm herself.

I thought the worst.

"Your dad . . . ?"

"He's okay," she managed to say. "But . . ."

We stared at each other for a few seconds, my mind racing, Caitlin seemingly unable to speak.

I waited and finally she drew a breath and let it out slowly.

"Dad's decided to retire," Caitlin said.

I relaxed a bit, thinking this was a good thing.

"The doctor insisted," she said. "Dad can't handle the stress of running the store. Only now . . ."

Or maybe this wasn't a good thing.

"What?" I asked, my anxiety spiking again.

"Now, Dad's ready for me to take over the store, like we always planned."

Okay, so it was a good thing.

Caitlin drew herself up, squared her shoulders, and stretched her mouth into a big smile.

"I wanted you to be the first to know," she said, forcing her smile wider. "We've set a date."

I just stared at her.

"Scott and me. We've set a date," she went on. "A wedding date. I'm getting married."

CHAPTER 12

"Well, congratulations," I managed to say.

"I know," Caitlin gulped. "Isn't it . . . wonderful?"

We were in the sewing studio. After she'd broken the news outside on Main Street, I'd insisted we come here so I could get all the details. Harriet was expecting me at the visitor center. I'd be late but I'd get there. My friend was more important.

"I mean, getting married is something every girl dreams of, right?" Caitlin asked, as she paced back and forth in front of me.

Before I could say anything, she went on.

"Being a bride. Having that one special day in your life. All women want that. Don't they?"

I couldn't say anything.

"Really, what could be better? A huge celebration. Friends and family together," she said.

I still couldn't say anything.

"The bridesmaids, the cake, the beautiful gown. Who wouldn't want that? Right?"

I wasn't sure who she was trying to convince—me or her. "What happened that you two decided to set a date?" I asked. "You and Scott have been engaged for a while now."

"Oh, yes, sorry." Caitlin massaged her forehead. "Sorry for not answering your text messages. I've been dealing with Dad. Mom is excited. She's waited for months, so she wanted to get things going. And Scott's mom, she doesn't have a daughter. She's anxious to help with plans."

"Sounds as if you'll have lots of input on everything," I said.

Caitlin seemed not to hear me. "I mean, really, it had to be done. Right? Dad and his heart problems. And the doctor. He's said for months that it's too stressful for Dad. He should retire. So this is for the best. Right?"

"Is it?"

"It needs to happen." Caitlin drew a breath. "It needs to. It's the best for everyone."

I wasn't so sure. Maybe for Caitlin's dad. But Caitlin herself?

"Your dad is really going to step back from running the store?" I asked.

"Yes, and I'm taking over. Completely. Officially. That's the whole point of setting the wedding date. Dad wants me to be settled, ready to assume the responsibility of running the store."

"Scott is excited?" I asked.

She looked lost for a moment. "Oh, yes. He is. I guess. Probably."

"You haven't talked to him about it?"

"Sure. I did. Dad insisted I call him right away. So, yes. Yes. Scott's . . . happy about it," Caitlin said. "Neither of us thought it would be this soon. But Dad needs to retire. His health depends on it. And Mom wants to travel."

"When's the wedding?" I asked.

"Soon."

"You don't know the date?" I asked.

"I wrote it down . . . somewhere." Caitlin massaged her temples with her fingertips. "But it's soon. I mean, there's no reason to wait. Dad can retire. Mom can finally go places. And it all depends on me getting married."

I wasn't sure if this was pre-wedding jitters or if something else was going on.

"You're sure about this?" I asked.

She drew a deep breath and let it out slowly.

"Yes," she said, and sounded calm for the first time since she'd stopped me on Main Street. "And I want you to be in the wedding. You will, won't you? Please say you will."

"Of course."

Caitlin heaved a sigh of relief and threw her arms around me in a quick hug. I wished I'd seen her smile once in this conversation, but she hadn't.

"I've got to go," she said. "Lots to do."

"I want to know everything," I said. "Keep me informed."

Caitlin hurried out of the sewing studio. I stood there for a few minutes trying to take everything in. I'd wondered before if Caitlin was truly committed to marrying Scott. They'd been engaged forever—long before I moved to Hideaway Grove—and they'd moved no closer to actually getting married.

A wedding was a huge undertaking and tons of things had to be arranged, and setting the date had been sprung on her unexpectedly. Maybe that was the reason for the odd vibe I'd picked up from Caitlin. Or maybe—

Mitch.

My heart sank. He was completely in love with Caitlin. How would he react when he learned that she'd set the date—and it was soon.

I dithered for a moment, not sure if I should tell Mitch myself now, before he heard it from someone in casual conversation. Or maybe I should stay out of it. It wasn't my news to tell.

No way could I let Mitch be blindsided by this news, I decided.

I yanked my phone out of my pocket. I almost called, but decided he'd likely not want an audience when he found out. I sent him a text message, a simple thought-you'd-want-to-know kind of thing and added that I was available anytime if he wanted to talk. I doubted he'd take me up on my offer.

I left the sewing studio and headed for the visitor center, glad that my day couldn't get any worse.

"You want me to—what?"

I think I said that louder than I should have.

Not that anyone noticed.

I was in the visitor center with Harriet and all that was left of the staff—Gloria and Janine.

Gloria sat at the desk near the luxe cabinet. She had on a striking coral pantsuit, accessorized with what looked to be expensive jewelry. Atop the desk sat the shopping bag— now empty—I'd seen her carrying toward the post office earlier; I saw now that it was a designer tote by Coach.

Janine stood in front of the counter dressed in her usual uniform of a butterscotch blazer and matching beret. Today she'd added a beige midi-length skirt, flats, and, for some reason, ankle socks.

The only thing I noticed about Harriet was her scowl— worse than usual.

It seemed the three of them had gotten their heads together before I arrived and come up with a plan, a plan that relied solely on me.

"It will be delightful!" Janine declared. "Just what we need!"

The last time I'd seen her, she'd vowed to come up with something to boost morale. I never thought it would hinge on me.

"You want me to make vests?" My words came out in a strangled whisper while my mind grappled with the idea.

"It was my idea," Janine declared, looking pleased with herself.

"For everybody?" I asked.

"It will give us a sense of unity," Janine went on.

My sewing skills were minimal.

"We'll look so smart when we're going through town, giving tours," Janine said.

I didn't know how to make a vest.

"After all, we're ambassadors. We should look the part!"

Vests were complicated. A lining. Buttonholes. How many buttons? A pocket? What type of fabric? And they would have to actually fit the wearer. I didn't know how to fit a garment. Clothing designers went to specialized schools to learn those things. I had a business degree.

"Well, I don't know," Gloria said. "Appearance is everything. But I'm not sure vests are the way to go."

I suddenly liked Gloria a lot.

"I think we'll look stunning," Janine declared.

"Of course," Gloria said. "It would be worth a try."

My affection for Gloria took a nosedive.

Janine gasped. "Oh, I know! We'll all get matching berets, too!"

No way was I wearing a beret. Not for a part-time job that paid minimum wage and would leave me with hat hair.

"Making vests would be a major undertaking for me," I said, and managed to sound composed.

Harriet's scowl deepened.

"I'm not sure how many I would have to make," I went on. "Are Paige and Kendall coming back to work? Will they be replaced? Are you hiring someone new to fill their positions?"

"I haven't heard from either of them," Harriet reported.

"That's why we need to do something to up our morale," Janine insisted.

I glanced at Gloria hoping she'd chime in. She said nothing.

I really didn't like her now.

"Morale could use a boost," Harriet agreed.

I racked my brain, desperately trying to come up with another reason not to be saddled with figuring out how to make vests. Finally, it hit me.

"Vests would be very expensive to make," I said.

Harriet seemed to shift gears, now considerably less worried about morale and more concerned about dipping into the visitor center's limited budget.

She thought for a moment and finally said, "Check into it, Abbey. Get me an estimate on the cost of sewing the vests. We'll move forward if it seems feasible."

"I can't wait to see what you make for us, Abbey! I'm off!" Janine twirled across the room, then dashed out the front door.

I wasn't on the clock, so I was free to go, but I didn't want to leave and take a chance of Janine seeing me on the street. I wasn't up to hearing more about her morale-boosting idea—which had definitely done nothing to lift my spirits.

The phone rang. Harriet answered it. Gloria still sat at the desk, the luxe log open in front of her, flipping the pages. I was tempted to ask her how in the world she'd come up with her system of tracking the valuable lost-and-found items, but she guarded the log and the items so closely I doubted she'd tell me.

Still, I didn't want this moment to be lost. I'd put Gloria on my mental suspect list for, really, no good reason. She was supposed to be here that morning and she wasn't. So what? Maybe I could find out.

I drifted across the room and stopped next to Gloria's desk, confident that I made the move look casual. She closed the log.

"Have you heard anything from Paige or Kendall?" I asked.

Gloria crossed her arms across the log. "Of course. I contacted both of them. You know, we're like family here."

"Do you think they'll come back to work?" I asked.

"I certainly hope so."

"Are you staying?" I asked.

Gloria gave me an indulgent smile. "Why would you even ask that?"

"The vests," I said. "I have to know how many we'll need so I can give Harriet an accurate estimate."

Gloria nodded slowly. "Oh, of course, I'll stay. You couldn't get me out of here if you tried."

"You're okay being here, even though Eleanor was murdered in the storage room?" I asked.

"Oh, that." Gloria waved away my words.

I noticed her nails were done and she wasn't wearing her wedding ring. She was a widow so she didn't have to, but I knew a lot of women did.

"You're not afraid to be here?" I asked.

"Not in the least," she declared.

Gloria's vague answers didn't inspire me to remove her from my suspect list. I decided to push a little harder.

"It was lucky you were late getting here that morning," I said. "What happened?"

"Divine intervention," she told me.

She said it so quickly I got the feeling she truly believed it—or she'd rehearsed.

"Abbey?" Harriet called, as she hung up the phone. "What's the latest on the dish ladies' tour?"

There was no *latest* on the dish ladies, that I knew of, but I grabbed the calendar from the top of the file cabinet and checked.

"Nothing new," I reported.

"And the bridal show?"

I looked again. "No changes."

The phone rang and Harriet answered. I decided it was a good time to leave.

Outside, evening shadows stretched across Main Street. Stores and shops would close soon. Folks ambled toward the restaurants and cafés.

Hideaway Grove was winding down for the day, but I was spun up. Everything I was involved with was crowding my mind—Eleanor's murder, Owen possibly cheating on his longtime girlfriend, Caitlin's wedding, vests I had no idea how to make. Uppermost in my thoughts, though, was Mitch.

I hadn't heard back from him since I shared the news about Caitlin's upcoming marriage. I wondered how he was handling it.

As I passed Eagle Avenue, I glimpsed the sign for the Night Owl Bar and wondered if Mitch was there. Maybe he could use a friend. Maybe he'd want to talk. I decided to take a chance.

When I got inside, I didn't see him. Zack sat at the bar, off-duty, a bottle of beer in front of him.

This required a very different sort of conversation.

Zack looked up as I approached. I sidled up next to him and leaned close.

"Want to talk about murder?"

CHAPTER 13

"Could we talk about sex instead?" he asked.

I ignored Zack's question and went to the booth at the rear of the bar where we usually sat. He signaled the bartender, then joined me carrying his beer bottle.

"Has the sheriff come up with anything new in Eleanor's death?" I asked.

"I guess that's a 'no' on the sex talk," Zack said, and settled onto the bench across from me.

A lock of his dark hair fell onto his forehead and a shadow of whiskers covered his jaw. He looked handsome in the bar's dim light. Still, I wasn't going to talk about sex with him—not at the moment, anyway.

"The sheriff. Has he come up with something?" I asked.

Zack hesitated. Maybe he wanted to insist he drive the conversation. Or maybe something else was going on. I couldn't be sure.

He sipped his beer and deliberately set it aside, then looked across the table at me.

"Yes," Zack said. "As a matter of fact, he has."

My spirits rose. "What?"

"He got some of the lab reports back." He glanced away, then looked at me again. "The only fingerprints on the shears—the murder weapon—are yours."

The news hit me hard. "You realize what this means?"

"Yes. We're never going to talk about sex."

"Someone sneaked into my sewing studio, stole the shears with my name on them, and was careful not to leave their own prints," I said, my outrage growing. "Someone is trying to frame me."

Really, I'd known that all along, but I hadn't wanted to face it. Now I had no choice.

"Who would do that to me?" I exclaimed. Then something else occurred to me. "I've been looking for someone who didn't like Eleanor. I should have been looking for someone who didn't like *me*."

Zack dropped his beer bottle on the table with a thud. "You're not supposed to be investigating anyone or anything."

I wasn't going to get into it with him.

"What else?" I asked. "Please tell me Sheriff Grumman has clues, evidence, a suspect—besides me."

"The investigation is ongoing."

I could tell he was annoyed with me for investigating Eleanor's death, but I kept pushing.

"Has he questioned Kendall?" I asked.

"Why would he?"

"Does he know she left town in a hurry—within hours, apparently, of Eleanor's murder?"

Zack paused, giving me my answer.

The bartender appeared at our booth and placed my mug of beer in front of me. I thanked him and took a long drink.

"How about Gloria?" I went on. "She was supposed to be at the visitor center that morning. She showed up late. It wasn't like her to be late. Where was she?"

"Have you come up with . . . say . . . a motive for either of these people to have murdered Eleanor, framing you in the process?" Zack asked, sounding too reasonable to suit me at the moment.

I hadn't, of course. All I had was suspicion and nothing to back it up.

"You think Gloria murdered Eleanor because of that squabble over the scissors—shears?" he asked.

"Maybe," I told him, though I knew it sounded petty.

"How about Kendall?" he asked.

"That morning, she just seemed to appear in the storage room out of nowhere. Then she left town without a word of explanation—not even to her roommates. Why would she do that unless she had something to hide?"

Zack nodded slowly and sipped his beer. Obviously, he recognized that my suspicions were almost completely unfounded, but had the good sense not to say it out loud.

I wasn't done yet.

"Rayna," I said. "Rayna Newberg. Eleanor's niece. She works at Birdie's."

"What about her?"

"She and Eleanor had an argument, a huge argument, early that morning, the morning Eleanor was murdered," I said.

"How do you know?"

"I went to see her at her house," I explained. "I was concerned about her."

"What did they argue about?"

"Eleanor insisted Rayna fight her landlord on her rent increase," I said.

"Lots of folks in town have a rent increase," he said. "No one else has been murdered."

"Okay, maybe Rayna doesn't have much of a motive to murder Eleanor, but—"

"Actually, she does."

Zack paused, as if debating whether to continue. I held my breath, waiting, thinking that if he didn't tell me what he knew—and quick—I might go across the table after him.

"This will be all over town soon, so I'm not speaking out of turn," Zack said. "Rayna isn't going to have to worry about her rent going up. Eleanor left her house to Rayna."

"She—what?"

Zack nodded.

I had trouble grasping what he'd said.

"Eleanor has children—stepchildren. They don't live in Hideaway Grove and she and Rayna were close, but to leave her house to Rayna? That's a huge gift," I said.

"Plus, the house is paid for. No mortgage."

No, it wasn't a huge gift, I realized. It was a blessing. A home to live in—a nice home, a home she would own—that wouldn't take a chunk of money out of her budget every month. Rayna had told me she was struggling financially, especially facing the increase in her rent. She certainly wouldn't have to worry about her budget now.

"Did Rayna know?" I asked.

"She admitted it to the sheriff, which gives her—"

"—the perfect motive for murder."

Zack and I stared at each other, both of us thinking the same thing. Rayna had motive and opportunity, making her a prime suspect.

"Rayna and Eleanor. They argued early?" he asked. "How early?"

I thought back to my conversation with Rayna at her house, the morning she'd been so upset about Eleanor's death.

"First thing, before either of them left for work. Rayna told me she was furious with Eleanor. She was a crusader, always righting a wrong, according to Rayna, and Rayna was sick of it," I said. "Does the sheriff know?"

"I'll make sure he does."

A tiny tremor of relief went through me, thinking that Sheriff Grumman might actually focus his investigation on someone other than me.

"But there's still those scissors—shears," Zack pointed out. "And your fingerprints."

My anxiety spun up again.

"Why would Rayna do that?" I wondered. "Why would she want to frame me?"

"Maybe she wanted to point a finger at *somebody*, not you in particular."

I'd like to think that were true—and maybe it was. Maybe, too, it would be better if I kept focused on finding Eleanor's murderer. If I found the killer, I'd know the answer to my question.

All these thoughts, speculations, and questions about murder seemed to weigh heavily upon me. I'd had enough oppressive thoughts for one evening. I wanted to talk about something different.

"What do you know about Owen Humphrey?" I asked.

"He wasn't murdered. Why are we talking about him?"

I wasn't going to tell Zack about Lily's concern that Owen was cheating on her sister. But he and Owen worked together. Maybe he knew something.

"Is he still seeing Willow?" I asked.

Zack paused with the beer bottle halfway to his lips, then set it down again and frowned.

"Why are you asking?" he demanded.

So much for my subtle interrogation tactic.

"I was just making conversation," I said with a casual shrug. "Do you know if he and Willow are—"

"No. I don't know. I don't know anything about them," Zack insisted.

"You know something," I realized.

"No." He shook his head.

"Yes, you do. Tell me what's going on."

Zack gave me his serious-deputy face—which was kind of hot—and didn't say another word.

"Okay, fine," I said with just enough attitude he'd be assured his refusal didn't suit me. "Then let's talk about marriage."

"Marriage?" His eyes widened. "We haven't even talked about sex yet."

"Caitlin and Scott set a wedding date," I said.

"About time. I don't know what they were waiting—" Zack sighed heavily. "Mitch."

Obviously, I wasn't the only one who was aware of Mitch's feelings for Caitlin.

"I feel bad for him," I said.

"He should have made a move a long time ago. Too late now."

"He was trying to do the right thing and respect Caitlin's engagement."

"And look where it got him."

I couldn't disagree.

We talked for a few more minutes, mostly about what was happening in town, until we finished our beers, then left the Night Owl together. At the corner we paused. The streetlamps had come on and traffic was light on Main Street. I wondered if Zack would ask me to have dinner with him, but he didn't. It suited me fine. All our talk about murder seemed to have dampened our time together.

Maybe we should have talked about sex.

"I've got things to work on at the sewing studio," I said.

Zack nodded, grasped my elbow lightly, checked traffic, and we crossed the street. Outside Sarah's Sweets, we murmured a good-bye. I went inside. Anna from the thrift shop dashed in behind me. The bakery would close in a few minutes. No customers were there. When I glanced out the door, Zack was gone.

"Am I too late?" Anna asked. "Don't tell me I'm too late. I can't face this evening without at least a dozen of your sugar cookies."

Aunt Sarah and Jodi stood behind the display counter, looking befuddled.

"What's going on?" I asked.

They seemed to snap out of their trance at once.

"Just the darndest thing," Aunt Sarah mused.

"Odd," Jodi agreed.

"Helen was just in here," Aunt Sarah explained. "You know Helen. From the bank."

Helen was the assistant manager at the only bank in Hideaway Grove. I knew her well enough to make casual conversation. I'd considered inviting her to my pillowcase dress parties but hadn't done it.

Every time I saw her, honestly, I was a bit envious. She wore business suits, low-heeled pumps, and minimal jewelry—all conservative, in keeping with her position, but with a sense of style. Her appearance reminded me of the big dream I'd had in college of working at a huge Los Angeles firm. She seemed to be thriving. I hadn't.

"I mentioned Eleanor's murder and she didn't say one word about it," Jodi said, pulling a pink bakery box from under the counter. "You know everybody is talking about it."

"Not only did she not say anything, but she sort of froze," Aunt Sarah said. "It seemed like a strange reaction."

"I certainly didn't mean to upset Helen by bringing up Eleanor's death." Jodi took sugar cookies from the display and placed them in the box. She passed it over the counter to Anna. "I had no idea they were close friends."

"They're not." Anna opened the box and helped herself to a cookie.

Everybody turned to her, waiting.

Anna gulped down the cookie. "Just the other day, I saw them arguing outside the drugstore. Not that I was spying, or anything, but they were right across the street from my shop."

"What happened?" I asked.

"Helen was heading toward the bank—I think she was on her lunch hour—and Eleanor came out of the drugstore at the same moment. There they were, suddenly face-to-face on the sidewalk, and Eleanor lit into Helen."

We all gasped.

Anna started in on another cookie. "Eleanor and Helen both raised their voices. It got heated."

"What were they arguing over?" I asked.

"I don't know what it was about, exactly. They were too far away so I couldn't hear what was being said. But it was obvious that Helen did not appreciate Eleanor's comments," Anna reported. "Helen told her so, then stomped away in a huff."

We all looked at each other, stunned.

"I certainly hope their confrontation didn't get back to Mr. Jarvis," Aunt Sarah said.

Mr. Jarvis was the bank manager. He was in his fifties, always dressed in a dark suit, always scowling. He reminded me of a high school principal, constantly on guard, waiting for someone to break a rule so he could pounce.

"He runs a tight ship," Anna said. "Not sure I'd want to work under those conditions."

"Helen is so sweet," Aunt Sarah said. "Every time I go into the bank, she's just as pleasant as she can be. I wonder why Eleanor confronted her."

"You know . . ." Jodi tapped her chin, as if recalling something. "I was in the bank last week and Helen was at her desk. I could see she was not happy with what was going on."

"She was talking to Eleanor?" I asked.

"No. It was Gloria," Jodi said. "I couldn't hear what was being said. But Helen was definitely not liking whatever they were discussing."

"Something to do with Gloria's husband's estate?" Aunt Sarah speculated.

"It's been a few months since he died. Mr. Schwartz was handling everything," Jodi said.

Mr. Schwartz was the most respected attorney in Hideaway Grove. He and his staff were extremely professional and knowledgeable, plus he was just as nice as he could be. Everyone thought highly of him.

"Helen's job must be stressful at times," Aunt Sarah said. "Dealing with customers, who are really friends and neighbors, and their financial situations. We all face difficult times, occasionally. That must put Helen in a tough spot."

"She has to be careful not to offend anyone," Jodi said.

"Or rile Mr. Jarvis," Anna added.

No way would I want to be Helen working under those conditions. But at the moment I was focused on her confrontation with Eleanor. Something had happened to bring about their heated discussion on a public street, in broad daylight, for everyone to witness.

I needed to find out what it was.

CHAPTER 14

"Abbey, I'd like you to meet our new employee," Harriet announced.

I was seated at one of the desks in the visitor center looking over the calendar. My first cup of morning coffee sat in front of me—no way was I ever drinking tomato juice again—and I was checking the schedule, getting a jump on the questions I knew Harriet would ask.

A new employee, I wasn't expecting.

"This is Marissa," Harriet said, then gestured to me. "And this is Abbey."

I'd never seen Marissa before, another reminder of how few people in Hideaway Grove I'd met so far. In a town where everyone seemed to know everyone, I was definitely behind the curve.

Marissa looked to be about my age, average height and build, with dark hair and eyes, dressed casually in jeans and a T-shirt. She didn't exhibit the usual first-day-on-the-job jitters. Instead, she looked bored.

"Welcome," I said. "Nice to meet you."

Marissa managed a slight shrug.

"What's going on with the dish ladies?" Harriet wanted to know, frowning.

I tapped the calendar in front of me. "No change."

"And the bridal show?" she asked.

"Both are still a go," I reported.

For some reason, Harriet's frown deepened. "Keep me informed."

"Of course," I said, and forced myself to sound patient and cooperative even though I hadn't finished my coffee.

"Abbey will show you around," Harriet said to Marissa, then pulled out her cell phone and walked away.

Marissa stared at me for a few seconds, then gestured to the calendar.

"You give tours?" she asked, looking confused.

"Yep. I sure do."

"I thought you were the cleaning lady."

"What? Who told you that?"

"I don't know." Marissa shrugged in don't-blame-me fashion. "That's what somebody said."

Who knew how gossip got started in a small town? Better she hadn't heard I was a murder suspect, I decided.

Marissa waved at the two empty desks. "Is this it? We're the only ones who work here?"

I didn't know if she was replacing Paige or Kendall, so I wasn't sure what to tell her.

"Gloria Marsh volunteers here," I said.

Marissa reeled back slightly. "That Gloria woman is here? Nobody told me she was here. I don't like her."

Gloria had been embroiled in controversary over her shears donation, but I didn't know how that incident could have reached Marissa.

"Why not?" I asked.

"Nobody likes her." Marissa gave a dismissive grunt. "Not now."

The telephone rang. Harriet was still on her cell so I passed the calendar to Marissa and said, "You should look this over, so you'll know what's coming up."

She took the calendar and walked away.

I grabbed the receiver. "Hideaway Grove visitor center."

"Hello," a woman said. "Could I speak with Gloria, please?"

Of course, Gloria wasn't in. Lately, she never seemed to be here when she was needed.

"She's not here," I said. "Can I help you?"

"Well, I don't know. I've been speaking with Gloria."

I recognized her voice. "Lois? Hi, this is Abbey. We spoke before about your wallet."

"Oh, yes. Yes, I remember."

When we'd talked before, I'd seen in the luxe log that the wallet Lois had lost while shopping in town with her daughter and friends had been returned to her several days ago. She should have gotten it by now.

"Did you get your wallet?" I asked.

I glanced at Marissa. She'd ignored my suggestion of looking over the calendar and had taken a seat at one of the other desks.

"Well, yes. I got a wallet," Lois said.

"Good news," I said.

"Well, no. Not really," Lois said. "I received a wallet. But it isn't my wallet."

"It's not?" I was startled and confused.

"My wallet was embroidered with my initials. A special order," Lois said, sounding confused, too. "This one, it belongs to someone else."

Marissa leaned back in the chair and put her feet up on the desk.

"I'm so sorry," I told Lois. "There must have been a mix-up in shipping."

If Gloria had sent the wrong wallet to Lois, hopefully

Lois's wallet was still in the luxe cabinet. Worst case, Gloria had sent Lois's wallet to someone else. But who? And how would we get it back?

"Is there an ID card in the wallet you received?" I asked.

"No. No, there's nothing in it." Lois sighed heavily. "I'm so disappointed. And upset. My wallet was a gift. A gift from my husband—my late husband. Very important to me."

Marissa pulled her cell phone from her pocket and took a selfie.

"My daughter asked about my wallet," Lois said, sounding more and more distraught. "I assured her it was being returned, but now *this* has happened. She's very busy. I don't want to involve her."

"I'll find out what happened," I told her. "I'll call you back as soon as I know something."

"You won't forget?" Lois asked. "My daughter will be very upset if I don't get my wallet back."

"I'll handle it," I said. "I promise."

Lois thanked me and I hung up the phone.

Of course, mix-ups happened, mistakes were made; we were all human. Still, I was a bit annoyed with Gloria.

"Is something wrong?" Harriet held her cell phone away from her ear and drilled me with a death-ray glare from across the room.

"Just a question about a lost wallet," I said. "I'll handle it."

I wasn't all that anxious to once more enter the maze that Gloria called her luxe log, but I wanted to get this problem solved. I grabbed the log from the top of the filing cabinet and flipped through it.

Harriet appeared beside me and looked over my shoulder.

"Let Gloria handle it," she told me. "You know how she gets."

I did, but I didn't much care.

"The woman who called is upset. I'd like to get this resolved right away," I said.

Marissa joined us. "You call that a log? Looks to me like some kindergartener thought it up."

I couldn't disagree.

"Or maybe some psycho," Marissa said.

It would be easier if I simply looked inside the luxe cabinet to see if Lois's wallet was there.

"We really need another key to the luxe cabinet," I said.

Harriet, apparently, didn't want my attempt to solve this problem to create another problem.

"Leave it for Gloria," she said, more insistent. "She'll handle it when she comes in again."

"I'll give her a call and see if she can come in now," I said.

I got my cell phone and called. Gloria answered right away, but I could barely hear her for the background noise, loud voices, odd tones, and an occasional rousing cheer.

"We need to get into the luxe cabinet," I told her.

"What? You need what?"

We went back and forth like that another time, and I finally gave up.

Obviously, Gloria wasn't home, which meant she couldn't come to the visitor center right away to resolve the issue with Lois's wallet. I checked the calendar and saw that she was scheduled to be in tomorrow.

"I guess it will have to wait," I said.

I turned to put the luxe log back on top of the filing cabinet and saw that Marissa was sitting at a desk again, now texting someone.

So far, I wasn't seeing how Marissa was going to be a real asset to the visitor center.

"That's Gloria," Marissa proclaimed, still fiddling with her phone. "Always on the move, always going . . . mostly to the same place."

"Where's that?" I asked.

She ignored my question. "Just another reason nobody likes her."

I didn't see Marissa and me becoming best buddies.

When my shift ended, I left the visitor center, glad to be out of there. I had a number of things to do and one of them I'd really let slide. I decided to tackle it first, head-on.

Inside Flights of Flowers, I spotted Lily at the back of the shop. When I walked up, her eyes got big.

"Oh, my gosh, I'm so glad you're here," she said, an urgency in her voice that bordered on panic.

"What happened?" I asked, my anxiety spinning up to match hers.

"Something awful." Lily glanced around as if to make sure no customers were close. "Owen and Willow were looking at engagement rings."

My anxiety morphed into confusion.

"That's awful?" I asked.

"Yes!" Lily glanced around once more and lowered her voice, her panic now turning into anger. "That Owen. He makes me so mad. Here he is cheating on Willow and he's looking at engagement rings with her."

Okay. I got it. And, yes, that was really bad.

Now I felt like a bad person, too, because Lily had asked me to find out what was really going on with Owen and I hadn't accomplished anything—well, one thing. When I'd been at the Night Owl with Zack and I'd asked him about Owen, he'd claimed he knew nothing, yet I had the distinct feeling that Zack was covering for him. I should have pushed and made Zack tell me everything he knew—though exactly how I'd have forced him to do that I wasn't sure.

"It's not right, leading her on like that," Lily said. "What have you found out? Where's he going? Who's he seeing?"

"I'm on it," I told her, and mentally vowed to do just that. "I'll let you know something soon."

I left the flower shop and headed for the bakery. Across

the street I saw that Peri was still working at the pet store. I wondered if Caitlin's dad knew she was there. For Caitlin's sake, I hoped he didn't.

The bell over the door chimed when I walked into Sarah's Sweets, and the delicious aroma of baked goods wafted over me. Geraldine stood in front of the display case, along with Valerie from the bookstore. Aunt Sarah and Jodi were behind the case looking slightly apprehensive.

"You're just in time," Geraldine declared when she saw me. "I have solved Hideaway Grove's problem."

Now I felt slightly apprehensive, too.

Geraldine stood a little taller. "You remember when I said we merchants simply could not continue to stake our financial futures on the whim of tour groups and conventions coming to town? Well, I know what we should do."

Everybody stared.

"Rodeo!" Geraldine announced.

Everybody continued to stare.

"We'll have the rodeo come to town," Geraldine said.

"But we don't have the facilities for that," Valerie said, confused.

"All those rugged, broad-shouldered men in their tight jeans, and those boots and cowboy hats . . ." Geraldine drifted off.

"How were things at the visitor center?" Aunt Sarah asked, anxious to change the subject.

"Or maybe one of those weightlifting competitions," Geraldine mused.

"I heard you were working there now," Valerie said. "You're the cleaning lady."

How the heck had that rumor gotten started? I wondered again.

"No cancellations, I hope," Jodi said.

"I'm thinking a big construction firm," Geraldine went

on, now slightly breathless. "Men with their tool belts and hard hats . . ."

"Everything is still on schedule," I said. "Pretty quiet there today, just a mix-up with one of Gloria's luxe items."

"Gloria?" Geraldine snapped out of her stupor. "That woman has changed, completely changed, since her husband died—and not in a good way."

She went on without anyone asking.

"Gloria was in my shop the other day, which surprised me." Geraldine pursed her lips. "Since Reggie passed away, she's been doing her shopping *elsewhere*."

"So what happened?" I asked.

"Well, just as I was showing Gloria my nicest sweater set, Eleanor came into the shop," Geraldine said. "They took one look at each other, sort of like a stare-down. Then Gloria up and left—with me standing there holding the most gorgeous beaded sweater set I've ever carried."

Everyone seemed to mull over Geraldine's story.

"I'm not surprised," Valerie finally said. "Gloria can't get along with anyone—not even her own family. Wanda can't stand her."

"Her sister-in-law," Aunt Sarah explained, seeing the lost look on my face. "Gloria's husband's sister."

"There's always been animosity between Gloria and Wanda, and it's gotten worse since Reggie died," Valerie said. "I heard that Wanda was seen going into Mr. Schwartz's law office. I'll bet it's something to do with Reggie's will."

"I heard somebody say that Gloria drove her husband to an early grave with all her complaints and demands," Jodi reported.

Aunt Sarah gasped. "That's terrible."

"I heard the same," Valerie agreed.

"Reggie was as sweet as a man could be," Geraldine said. "I don't know how he managed to put up with Gloria."

"She's not exactly acting like a grieving widow," Valerie said. "She seems to be enjoying her life these days, going places and doing things."

I'd noticed that Gloria had upgraded her clothing and accessories. Seemed she wanted to look her best, whatever she was *doing* at those *places*.

"Spending Reggie's life insurance money, probably," Jodi said.

"How foolish," Aunt Sarah.

"All I know is that Gloria was ready to buy my lovely sweater set until Eleanor walked in," Geraldine declared. "They didn't like each other. That's for certain. And I lost a sale because of it."

I'd thought the conflict between Gloria and Eleanor stemmed from the scissors and shears donation. I realized now it was something more. But what had caused it? And where had it led? To murder?

CHAPTER 15

So far, Gloria hadn't shown up for her shift at the visitor center this morning. I'd been in the office for hours with no sign of her and no phone call explaining why she wasn't there, as expected, or when she intended to come in. The situation with Lois Atwater's lost wallet had been on my mind since yesterday, and I was anxious to get to the bottom of it.

"Still nothing from Gloria?" I asked.

Harriet, seated at the desk beside mine, shook her head. "Nothing."

"I really think we should get back to Lois about her wallet," I said, and managed to sound concerned rather than irritated.

"Gloria will handle it." Harriet rose from her desk. "I'm off."

Marissa sat at another desk concentrating on her phone, ignoring us.

"I'm meeting with the mayor," Harriet said.

"What's up?" I asked.

Several things—problems, actually—came to mind, few of

them anything that would benefit the visitor center or insure my continued employment.

"I feel it would be in the best interest of everyone concerned if we cancelled Lost and Found Day," Harriet said, sounding as if this was a grave decision she'd wrestled with all night—which she probably had. "I have to speak with Mayor Green, find out what she thinks."

Mayor Green, too, had the best interest of everyone uppermost in her mind. I wasn't sure how she'd feel about cancelling. It sent a message, one that our local merchants would likely spin up into considerably more than it was.

"I need your estimate on making vests for our employees," Harriet reminded me.

Honestly, I'd deliberately dragged my feet, hoping Harriet would come to her senses and realize that Janine's suggestion was a bad idea and forget the whole thing. Not so, apparently.

"I'm working on it," I said. It was a lie, but hopefully Harriet might still forget about it; she could use one less thing to stress about.

Harriet nodded, drew a breath, as if mentally preparing herself to face a firing squad, and left.

I wondered if she would end up discussing more than the future of Lost and Found Day with Mayor Green, such as the possibility that the visitor center should be closed. The phone hadn't rung all morning, no tourists had come in, so it seemed a definite possibility.

I glanced at Marissa still seated at the desk, completely focused on her phone, texting someone. While I was concerned that I might lose my job here, Marissa gave the impression that she couldn't have cared less.

Sitting here for several more hours until my shift ended with little to do wasn't a prospect I relished. Since Gloria's appearance at the office today seemed to be in limbo, I decided to take another run at figuring out her luxe log in the hope of figuring out what had caused the mix-up with Lois's wallet.

The log seemed as confusing as the last time I'd tried to decipher it when I opened it on my desk. Multicolored lines, arrows, highlighters traveled from page to page with no rhyme or reason I could understand. As Marissa had commented before, it looked as if it was written by a kindergartener—or a psycho.

Still, I refused to abandon my attempt to solve the mystery of Lois's wallet. She'd told me Gloria had informed her that her wallet had been shipped. It had gone somewhere—I just had to figure out where.

The best way to track down the wallet was to check with the other visitors who'd reported a lost wallet, I decided. Maybe one of them had received Lois's wallet instead of their own. Nice, if it could be that simple.

Since I didn't want to rely solely on Gloria's log, I grabbed a yellow legal pad from the desk drawer and started a list of the people I would contact. Flipping through the luxe log, best I could figure was that five visitors had reported losing their wallet while visiting Hideaway Grove.

I couldn't help but wonder what the heck was wrong with so many women that they couldn't keep track of their wallet—of all things. From the descriptions, these were all designer brands. I wasn't any sort of fashionista, but I knew they'd all cost a small fortune.

I began calling the names listed in the log, jotting down the pertinent info on my legal pad. Surprisingly, I got an answer at three numbers, all women, all of whom sounded older and were pleased to hear from me. Each of them told me they'd been informed—by Gloria, of course—that their wallet hadn't been turned in to the visitor center and they were now excited thinking I was phoning to let them know it had been recovered.

I felt bad because I'd gotten their hopes up, so I mentally scrambled and came up with the excuse that I was just letting them know that we were still watching for their lost item and would let them know if we located it. The women didn't seem any happier and I didn't feel any better.

I pushed on and phoned the last two entries in Gloria's log who had reported a lost wallet, got voicemails, and left a message asking them to call.

So far, I'd made absolutely no progress and was no closer to finding out who might have mistakenly received Lois's wallet—yet I'd managed to upset three very nice older ladies.

Maybe I should have waited for Gloria.

I paged through the log again, once more marveling at all the things visitors lost while in town. Even though I'd seen the year's worth of accumulated items in the bins in the storage room, looking at the individual log entries was stunning—handbags, watches, jackets, sweaters, phones, earrings, necklaces, eyeglasses, hats, wallets, toys, baby bottles, and on it went.

"Those ladies didn't get their stuff back, huh?" Marissa said.

I guess she'd been listening to my phone calls, which surprised me.

"Nope," I said.

"Figures . . ." Marissa slid deeper into the desk chair and turned back to her phone. ". . . with Gloria in charge."

She made it sound like I should have known better, which didn't make me feel any better—nor did it make me think I'd ever like Marissa any better.

I'd gotten up from the desk to return the luxe log to the top of the filing cabinet when the phone rang. To my surprise, Marissa answered it, but bumped her coffee cup, knocking it onto the floor. Coffee went everywhere.

A box of tissues sat on the front counter, but no way

would those things mop up the mess. I eyed the door leading to the storage room and the employees' break area where the paper towels were located. I shivered. I'd been there only when absolutely necessary since discovering Eleanor's body.

With a determined breath, I opened the door.

Only two lights burned, casting the storage room in deep shadows. The room was stuffy and still, since the big roll-up door hadn't been opened in days. A heavy silence hung over the room; no noise drifted in from the parking lot out back.

The image of Eleanor and that red stain on her chest slammed into my thoughts. I struggled to push it away.

The bins containing the found items had been shifted around, probably by the crime-scene techs as they'd gone about their investigation into Eleanor's death. I hoped Mayor Green would agree to cancelling Lost and Found Day.

Deputy Owen Humphrey drifted into my thoughts. He'd been so considerate when he'd arrived that morning, kind and gentle, attentive to me after the trauma of finding Eleanor's body. Hard to believe he was cheating on Willow.

Hard to believe, too, that Zack had been just the opposite. He'd explained his thoughts, his actions, and I understood them. Still . . .

I grabbed a roll of paper towels from the cabinet and dashed back into the office, closing the door with a thud.

The phone call Marissa had taken—questions about accommodating a disabled visitor—seemed to be winding down as I yanked a yard of paper towels off the roll and dropped to my knees, soaking up the spilled coffee.

The bell over the front door chimed as Marissa hung up the phone. Brooke walked in. She stopped at the counter and looked down at me.

"You're always trying so hard," she said, her ever-present fake smile in place, now with fake admiration added. "I know your aunt must be proud of you. Your parents, too."

"Do you need something?" Marissa asked, her tone suggesting that if Brooke did, in fact, need something, Marissa had no intention of helping her.

"Yes!" Brooke lit up, her eyes big and bright, her smile wide. "I have something to show you! Abbey, look at this."

I finished mopping up the spilled coffee, dropped the dripping paper towels into the trash can, and cleaned my hands from the disinfectant bottle on the desk. I walked to the front counter, and, for some reason, Marissa came, too.

Brooke swiped through several screens on her phone, then held it up.

"The design for my tote bags," she announced. "I know you're dying to see it."

Actually, I'd forgotten about it.

Picking up on my lack of enthusiasm, apparently, Brooke turned her phone toward Marissa.

"I'm doing totes for my friends," she said. "My husband and I are renewing our vows!"

Marissa frowned. "Somebody married you?"

"It's going to be—well, it's going to be the most fun event ever." Brooke flung out her arms. "We're reenacting Cinderella at midnight!"

Marissa and I stared at her.

"Picture it," Brooke went on. "My hair in a perfect, golden updo. I'll be wearing a gorgeous blue gown and glass slippers."

We didn't say anything.

"And my husband will be dressed like Prince Charming," Brooke said.

"You mean, in tights?" Marissa asked, frowning.

"Yes, of course," Brooke declared.

"A grown man wearing tights?" Marissa's frown deepened. "What happened? Did he lose a bet?"

"And then, *then*, at the stroke of midnight, I'll run down the stairs, lose my slipper, he'll find it, drop to his knees—"

"Did you catch him cheating on you?" Marissa asked.

"—he'll slide the slipper onto my foot—"

"Buy a sports car without talking to you?" Marissa asked.

"—take me into his arms, kiss me, and we'll live happily ever after," Brooke declared.

"I don't know about that," Marissa mused.

"So," Brooke said, holding her phone toward me again. "This is the design I want for my tote bags. I don't know how you think you're going to have a tote bag business when your sewing skills are so bad, but good for you that you keep trying. Really, it's just the sweetest thing. I kept my design as simple as I could. See?"

I didn't bother to look.

"I'll send you my design. I need ten of them, right away." Brooke pecked on her phone, then gave us a little finger wave. "Got to run."

She dashed out of the visitor center. Marissa and I stared after her.

"I hope whoever took out her brain saved it," Marissa grumbled.

Seemed Marissa and I might get along okay, after all.

Another hour crept by in near silence—no phone calls, no tourists—before Harriet returned from her meeting. She didn't look any happier than when she left. Not a good sign.

"How'd it go with the mayor?" I asked, putting some enthusiasm in my voice, as if that might make things better.

Harriet dropped her handbag on the desk and sighed heavily.

"She doesn't want to cancel Lost and Found Day," she reported. "We're postponing."

Kind of good news, I thought. If Mayor Green didn't want to cancel, she must believe the visitor center was important to Hideaway Grove and not likely to be shut down anytime soon. Still, I didn't relish the future possibility of spending hours in the storage room, sorting through the bins with the memories of finding Eleanor's body swirling through my head.

"Postponing until when?" I asked.

"I don't know." Harriet dropped heavily onto the desk chair. "I'll have to look at the calendar."

"I'll get it," I offered.

"No. I'll check it later."

Not good, I thought. Despite my optimism about remaining open, apparently something had gone on during Harriet's meeting with Mayor Green that was weighing on her mind.

When my shift finally ended, I left the visitor center, anxious for my day to get better. Ahead of me on the sidewalk I spotted the sign for Flights of Flowers, reminding me of the situation between Willow and Owen, which didn't help my mood.

Lily hadn't alerted me to Owen breaking a date with Willow—my cue to swing into action—but I decided to check things out for myself and, hopefully, come up with something.

I circled around the visitor center to the big parking lot out back. It was crowded, as always, with people coming and going and cars creeping through the aisles hoping to snag a close parking space.

The morning of Eleanor's murder slammed into my thoughts, even though I didn't want it to; perhaps it always would, every time I came here. Once more I wished I could remember something about that morning that would point me to her killer.

Near the rear entrance to the sheriff station, I pulled out my phone and checked Deputy Owen Humphrey's personal info that Lily had given me. I spotted his pickup parked at the back of the lot.

I saw Owen, in uniform, on duty, chatting with a man I

didn't recognize. Owen smiled and pointed. The man nodded and went on his way.

Owen seemed to be the nicest guy. If I found out he was cheating on Willow, I'd be almost as disappointed as Willow was likely to be.

The door to the sheriff station opened and Zack walked out, in uniform, on duty. My heart always did a little pitter-pat seeing him. Not this time. Not a *pitter*, maybe a barely discernable *pat*.

Zack didn't see me. I didn't walk over.

I left.

CHAPTER 16

Few customers were inside Connie's Fabrics when I walked in. The store was quiet, peaceful, as always. I liked coming here. My shift at the visitor center hadn't been much fun, nor had seeing Owen, then Zack outside the sheriff's station. The soothing effect of cloth, notions, and sundries was welcoming.

I roamed the aisles checking out the displays of thread, bias tape, and the bolts of fabric while Connie helped the customers select skeins of yarn. Connie owned the store. She was short, with dark hair, probably in her forties. I'd always found her to be as sensible as the clothes she usually wore.

When the customers finished their purchases and went on their way, I walked over to the checkout register. Connie looked troubled.

"You know, Abbey, if you had better sewing skills I would have given you a job here," she said, almost as if it were an apology.

I wasn't sure where this was coming from, and I guess my expression said as much because Connie went on.

"I don't mean to imply there's something wrong with working as a cleaning lady," she said.

This again. Good grief.

I decided to ignore the whole thing.

Connie had always been a lifesaver when I'd faced previous sewing challenges. I knew she could help me again.

"I need to ask you about making some vests," I said.

Her eyebrows rose. "Ambitious."

"I figured," I said, then told her about Harriet wanting me to give her an estimate on constructing vests for the visitor center employees.

"Janine's idea," Connie said. "Right?"

"Yep."

"What style of vest do you want to make?" she asked.

"I don't know."

"Darts? Decorative pockets? Pleats?"

"I don't know."

"You'll need everyone's measurements to size them correctly. How tight do you want the vest to fit?"

"I don't know."

Seeing that I was completely lost, Connie launched into a description of what would be required. I pulled out my cell phone and tapped out the list of things as she rattled them off: fabric in denim, canvas, cotton, or maybe corduroy; interfacing; buttons; thread; and, of course, a pattern. She knew her stock so well she gave me the prices without looking them up. The project was as complicated—and beyond me—as I'd suspected.

After a quick mental calculation, and adding in my labor, it seemed like a lot of money, more than I figured Harriet was willing to pay, hopefully.

"How many do you need to make?" Connie asked.

"Too many," I mumbled, and put my phone away. "Janine thought it might boost morale."

"Maybe it will help." Connie gave me a sympathetic

smile. "Must be uncomfortable working there now after . . . what happened."

"It is, and worrisome," I said. "Paige isn't likely to come back. Kendall left town. Harriet and the mayor decided to postpone Lost and Found Day. We have a new employee, but I'm not sure she'll last very long."

"Who?"

"Marissa . . . something," I said, unable to come up with her last name.

Connie shook her head, not able to come up with her name, either.

"We haven't been busy. I wonder if people are staying away because of . . . what happened," I said. "Honestly, I'm afraid the visitor center might have to close."

"Eleanor would be quite distressed if she knew she'd caused a problem there," Connie said. "She prided herself as upholding Hideaway Grove's highest standards and encouraged everybody to do the same."

I thought about Rayna and her argument with Eleanor about the increase in her rent.

"I'm not sure everyone was happy living up to Eleanor's expectations," I said.

"Her intentions were always good," Connie insisted. "Just look at the issue of the rent increase."

"You heard about Eleanor's argument with Rayna?" I asked, a little surprised.

"Rayna's rent is going up? Hers, too?"

"That's what I heard," I said.

"It's happening all over town."

I thought of Rayna and Peri, and the guy Kendall had been rooming with, all of them facing financial hardship, unsure how they'd pay more rent every month. Bad enough the three of them were dealing with the problem, but there were others?

"All the renters are upset, understandably so. No improvements have been made to any of the properties. Nothing justifies the increase," Connie said. "That's why Eleanor was organizing the renters. She wanted everyone to refuse to pay the increase."

"But Eleanor owned her home."

"She saw a wrong that needed to be righted, so she jumped in. That's the way she lived," Connie said.

"Could the renters do that? Simply refuse to pay the increase?" I asked.

Connie frowned. "I don't really know."

I wondered if Eleanor—or anyone—had asked Mr. Schwartz, Hideaway Grove's favorite attorney, the legalities of the issue.

"But you had to admire Eleanor's willingness to take on other people's problems," Connie said. "And her commitment to doing the right thing."

I wondered how much the owners of those properties had admired Eleanor's willingness and commitment.

The bell over the door clanged and two customers walked in. I thanked Connie for her help with the vests.

"Good luck," she said, and her tone indicated I'd need it.

I couldn't disagree.

I left the fabric shop and stood on Main Street for a moment. I spotted Anna outside her thrift shop sweeping the sidewalk. A mom and a little boy that I'd often seen around town went into Aunt Sarah's bakery; he was a cute little guy and she seemed like a devoted mother. Gloria, tote bag in hand, headed for the government center. Through the display window at Flights of Flowers I saw Lily chatting with a customer.

Everything seemed calm and peaceful, as always. Too calm and peaceful? Maybe it was my imagination, but there seemed to be fewer cars and tourists in town lately.

Eleanor's murder flew into my thoughts. I'd suspected the

news of her death might keep people away. Could that really be happening?

Connie had expounded on Eleanor's wonderful qualities, yet, somehow, she'd been murdered. How was that possible?

Maybe Rayna could tell me, I thought when I spotted her up ahead outside Birdie's Gifts and Gadgets.

"Hi, Rayna," I said when I walked up.

She jumped and whirled to face me. "Oh, goodness, you startled me."

The last time I'd seen Rayna was at her house the day her aunt had been murdered. She'd been an emotional mess, understandably, but didn't seem to have improved. Her puffy face and swollen eyes made me think she'd been crying and could burst into tears at any moment—not exactly the callous, hardened murderer I'd put at the top of my mental suspect list.

"I'm surprised you're working," I said, and nodded to the figurines she was adding to the display of merchandise positioned by the store's entrance.

"I took some time off, but I had to come back. This is my job. I'm expected to be here, no matter what." She threw a nervous glance through the door into the shop, then leaned closer and lowered her voice. "I'm doing the best I can but I'm getting blamed for . . . things."

"What kind of things?" I asked.

"I was told to watch out for certain . . . things," she said.

"What things?" I asked again.

"You know . . . *things*."

I had no idea what she was talking about.

"I'm not supposed to say," Rayna told me, and her distress amped up. "It's always something. I'm always getting the blame. But it's not my fault—I can't help what other people do or what they say. I'm trying hard—I really am. I'm afraid I'm going to get fired."

I didn't know who owned the gift shop, but I couldn't imagine whoever it was would actually fire Rayna. That sort of thing didn't happen in Hideaway Grove, usually.

"It's not easy to do your best work with that sort of thing hanging over your head," I said.

Rayna glanced around again. "It's always been that way here. But now . . . now I think I really might be fired."

Memories of the difficulties I'd endured at my job in Los Angeles hit me hard. I didn't like that Rayna—or anyone— had to go through it.

"Is there something I can do to help?" I asked.

She shook her head quickly. "I'm not supposed to talk about it."

I understood keeping work situations confidential, but she was so upset I wanted to make her feel better somehow.

"I hope you won't lose your job," I said. "But at least you don't have to worry about paying rent any longer."

Rayna gulped hard. "That's a real blessing. I don't know what I'd do if Eleanor hadn't left her house to me. It was always a comfort knowing I could count on that."

"You knew she was leaving her house to you?" I asked.

"Oh, yes. She put it in her will a long time ago. Mr. Schwartz handled it. He's such a nice man," Rayna said. "She has step-children, you know. They weren't close, but Eleanor thought they might be upset by her decision. She wanted me to know so I'd be prepared."

"That was very generous of her," I agreed.

"I certainly never wished anything bad would happen to Eleanor," Rayna said. "But, honestly, this couldn't have happened at a better time."

Had Rayna insured that now was the *better time*? Had she killed Eleanor to get ownership of her house right away instead of waiting for nature to take its course?

I definitely thought she could have.

How would I prove it?

"I'm going to need a taste tester soon," Jodi called when I walked into the bakery.

No customers were there, just Jodi at the work island in the kitchen. Whatever she was baking smelled delicious.

"It's something new. For the bridal show," Jodi said. "You're not going to be able to stop eating this."

I mentally pictured the waistband of my favorite jeans fitting tighter and tighter.

"Where's Aunt Sarah?"

"She had something to take care of," Jodi said. "I'll let you know when this is ready to taste."

From the aroma filling the bakery, I'd have to muster all my willpower not to eat too much. Somehow.

Jodi looked up from the work island and gave me an aren't-you-lucky smile. She nodded toward the sewing studio. "You have a visitor."

I slid the pocket doors open and saw Mitch at the windows, his toolbox on the floor beside him.

"I wanted to finish up with the repairs," he said.

"Great. Thanks."

I dropped my tote bag on the cutting table, thinking about what I needed to work on next, and realized why Mitch had returned to the repairs on the windows. A wave of sadness wafted through me. I knew what he wanted.

"No word from Caitlin lately," I said. "I guess she's pretty busy with the—"

I almost said *wedding* but caught myself.

"—with the store and her dad," I said.

He nodded out the window toward the pet store across the street. "I haven't noticed her over there."

I could tell he'd put some effort into making it sound casual.

"Peri's been managing the store," I said. "I hope Caitlin's dad doesn't find out. You know how he is."

Mitch nodded, then turned back to the windows. I saw him gaze outside and figured he was looking at the pet store again.

My heart broke a little more for him.

"So," I said, trying to put a little cheer into my voice. "What's happening with that big job you mentioned?"

Mitch paused for a moment, seemingly shifting mental gears, bringing himself back to the moment.

"A client I've worked for before," he said. "He bought a chateau near Paris and wants me to handle some of the renovations."

I'd been to Paris during some of my teenage summers when my parents had dragged me from museum to museum throughout Europe. Restoring a chateau sounded way better.

"Are you going to do it?" I asked.

"I don't know."

Mitch shrugged and turned back to the window repairs. Seemed he knew he should stay busy. I should, too.

I needed to finish a few more tote bags to complete the order I'd gotten from the gift shop chain, so I checked the details and set up the embroidery machine. I selected the requested design and loaded the colored threads, and off it went. I still had Brooke's totes to do but, so far, I hadn't been able to bring myself to look at the design she'd come up with.

"Done," Mitch said a few minutes later. He stepped back from the windows. "Want to give them a try?"

I went over and closed, then opened, each of the windows. They glided smoothly up and down.

"Perfect," I said.

"I'll stop by the hardware store and get screens for them."

"Thanks," I said. "Send me your bill."

He shrugged as if the work were nothing, grabbed his toolbox, and we left the sewing studio together.

"Just in time," Jodi called.

She walked out of the kitchen with a dozen petit fours on a tray. They were drenched in yellow and pink icing and were decorated with swirls of mint green and lavender.

"For the bridal show," she reminded me.

"Very elegant," I said.

"Almond cake with buttercream icing. I filled some with apricot, some have strawberry, and a few are lemon," Jodi explained. "Also, chocolate cake with raspberry filling."

I selected a delicate pink one and nibbled the corner. The cake was moist, the icing smooth, and the strawberry filling was just sweet enough to weaken my knees.

"Oh, my God . . ." I almost swooned.

Mitch selected a yellow one—lemon, I figured—and popped it into his mouth.

"Good," he said, then took another one.

"What do you think?" Jodi asked me.

I ate another tiny bite.

I was pretty sure I felt my waist expand.

"Delicious," I said.

Jodi smiled proudly and eased the tray toward Mitch. He took two more. I'm sure he hadn't the slightest bit of concern about the waistband of his jeans.

Men. I swear.

"Tastes great to me," he said, then turned to me. "I'll let you know about the screens."

"Thanks."

Mitch grabbed another petit four and headed out of the bakery. Jodi and I watched him leave, then both of us sighed and snapped back into the moment.

"You had another visitor, earlier today," Jodi said, frowning. "Sheriff Grumman came by."

Definitely not a visitor I wanted to see.

"What now?" I asked.

"He claimed he just wanted to ask you something. He wouldn't say what it was about, but I'm sure I know."

I was sure, too.

True, I wasn't making much progress finding Eleanor's killer. But if the sheriff had been here to question me again— back to square one, essentially—that must mean he wasn't making much progress, either.

Not good.

I couldn't wait for him to ask more questions, look for clues, wait for lab reports, and attempt to gather information that would lead to Eleanor's murderer. I had to handle it myself. That meant I had to do more. I had to do better.

While Sheriff Grumman had the authority, access to information, the assistance of deputies, crime-scene techs, and forensic experts, I had something he didn't. It was time to put my secret weapon to use.

Time to schedule a party.

CHAPTER 17

What was I going to do if this place closed, I thought as I stood at the counter in the visitor center watching the front door that hadn't opened all morning and glancing every few seconds at the phone that had yet to ring. This job was my only consistent source of income. How would I make my car payment? Pay Aunt Sarah rent? Cover my other bills?

As bad as my L.A. job had been, at least I didn't have to worry about making ends meet.

I glanced around. Marissa sat at one of the desks, slouched in the chair, tapping on her phone. Harriet hid behind her laptop. She'd never brought it into the visitor center before. I wondered if she was applying for a job.

"Did Gloria come in yesterday?" I asked.

I'd seen her heading toward the government center yesterday when I left Connie's Fabrics.

Neither Harriet nor Marissa responded.

"Did she check on the lost wallet? Lois Atwater's wallet?" I asked.

Marissa rolled her eyes. "She was here, carrying on about

that tote bag of hers being so heavy, looking at me like she thought I ought to volunteer to take it to the post office for her."

"Yes," Harriet said, not bothering to look up from her laptop. "Gloria checked on it."

"I don't know about that," Marissa grumbled. "All I saw her do was scribble in that so-called luxe log of hers."

The phone rang. Harriet grabbed it before I could get to it.

"Two of those people called you back yesterday," Marissa said.

It took me a second to realize what she was saying and finally remembered I'd left messages for two tourists who'd reported losing their wallets while in town.

"What did they say?" I asked.

She gazed at her cell phone for another few seconds, then opened her desk drawer and pulled out two slips of paper.

She held them out. "They said Gloria told them their wallets hadn't been turned in."

I took the messages from her, slightly annoyed that she'd neglected to hand them over when I arrived. I recognized the names of the two women I'd left voicemails with. As Marissa had said, they'd stated they never got their wallets back.

I'd hoped that the shipping mix-up with Lois's wallet was just that—a mix-up, and that some other woman had received Lois's wallet. Not so, apparently. Still, I couldn't help but think that if Gloria had made one mistake, she might have made others. I really needed to figure out that luxe log of hers or, at least, get a look inside the luxe cabinet.

Another thought—this one more concerning—came to me. With so many women losing their wallets while visiting Hideaway Grove, did that mean a pickpocket was on the loose, preying on unsuspecting tourists?

My conversation with Rayna came back to me. Had the owner of Birdie's Gifts and Gadgets been upset with her for not watching the sales floor and the stock more closely? Had she been referring to a shoplifter?

Hideaway Grove had always seemed so safe, so secure, so friendly, but now I wondered if criminals were among us— other than the person who'd murdered Eleanor, of course.

Harriet bolted to her feet so fast her chair flew back and hit the wall. She stared straight ahead, her mouth open, her face gone white, clutching the telephone receiver in her fist.

Startled, I jumped up, too. Even Marissa got up.

"What? What happened?" I hurried to the desk, visions of news of a death, a catastrophic fire, a horrific auto accident blooming in my head.

Harriet stood frozen for a few more seconds, then shook her head slowly.

"The dish ladies," she whispered.

A tsunami of dread hit me.

"Who?" Marissa asked.

"They've . . ." Harriet gulped. "They've postponed."

"Oh no," I said.

Marissa frowned. "What are dish ladies?"

"They've postponed," Harriet said again, as if in a trance.

I pried the telephone receiver out of her hand and returned it to the cradle.

"But they didn't cancel, right?" I asked.

"No," Harriet admitted. "Several of them are ill. That's what she said. But . . . but you know what this means."

"Maybe they really are ill," I offered.

"You know what this *means*," Harriet shrieked. "First Lost and Found Day, now the dish ladies. If the bridal show cancels—"

Harriet's knees gave out. I grabbed the desk chair and rolled it under her. She plopped down.

"Can you get her some water?" I asked Marissa.

She drew back. "I'm not going into that storage room. That place gives me the heebie-jeebies."

It gave me the heebie-jeebies, too, but I dashed through the door and grabbed a bottle of water from the refrigerator in the employee break area. When I got back into the office, Harriet had flung herself back in her chair and her eyes were closed.

"I think she's dead," Marissa said.

"*What?*"

I'm pretty sure I screamed that.

I must have because Harriet lurched forward, frantic.

"Somebody else *died*?" she shouted.

"No, no," I told her. "Nobody died. Everybody is fine."

"I'm not fine," Marissa insisted.

I opened the bottle of water and pressed it into Harriet's hand.

"Well, now, maybe I'm getting better," Marissa said.

I saw that she was looking out the front window at Main Street. Deputy Owen Humphrey stood on the sidewalk looking sharp in his uniform, gazing thoughtfully down the block.

"That is one fine-looking man," Marissa declared.

I was annoyed with her—not that I needed another reason.

"He's dating someone," I told her. "They're serious."

"Nothing wrong with what I'm doing," Marissa said, defensive now.

Men walked past our big windows all day. Owen was the only one Marissa had ever commented on. I wondered why.

Or maybe I knew why.

Cheddar jumped onto the windowsill as I double-checked the tote bags I'd completed for the gift shop order. He paced back and forth, ignoring the afternoon sun and the sounds of cars and voices that drifted in from Main Street.

"Well, hello," I said.

Cheddar sat down and curled his tail, looking at me. I would miss his visits when Mitch got the screens for the windows.

"How's your day going?" I asked, and walked closer.

He yawned, his jaws opening wide, and his eyes closing.

"You have company, huh?" I heard Caitlin's voice outside and spotted her on the sidewalk.

"You're welcome, too," I said. "Come on in."

She grinned. "I'll use the door."

Cheddar jumped into the sewing studio and a moment later, Caitlin came through the pocket doors.

"You've been on my mind," I said. "How's your dad?"

"Grumpy. Grouchy. The usual," she said. "But he's resting more than he ever has, following the doctor's orders . . . kind of."

"Must be hard on your mom."

"It is. That's why I've been helping." Caitlin gestured out the window. "Thank goodness Peri is managing the store. I've had to handle a few things but she's picking up everything quickly. She managed a store for a couple of years, somewhere near San Luis Obispo, I think. Plus, she has a business degree. She wants to open her own store, one day."

"Sounds like she's perfect for the job," I said.

I couldn't help thinking about the business degree I'd gotten that, so far, had landed me a job in Los Angeles that I hadn't been able to handle, a part-time job at the visitor center that was likely to close, and a tote bag business that wasn't going anywhere.

I wondered if Caitlin was remembering the art school she'd briefly attended before being yanked back to Hideaway Grove to help with the family pet store. During my childhood summers here, even at such a young age, Caitlin's artistic talent was obvious.

"How's the wedding prep going?" I asked.

"The—what?"

"The preparation for your wedding," I said.

Caitlin gave herself a little shake. "Oh, yes. Of course. It's coming along. Mom's loving it. Scott's mother, too."

"Let me know when you're shopping for your dress."

"Oh. That. Well, I already have a dress."

"You do?" I couldn't keep the disappointment out of my voice.

"I got it a long time ago," she explained. "When Scott and I first got engaged, Mom insisted we find a dress right away."

"I want to see it."

"Sure." Caitlin shrugged. "Mom wanted me to get something grand, so we found something she liked . . . finally. I'll bring it over."

Cheddar trotted across the sewing studio and rubbed against the rack where the finished pillowcase dresses hung.

"I think he's trying to tell you something," Caitlin said.

"Smart cat," I agreed. "I'm going to schedule another pillowcase dress party."

I didn't want to explain that I intended to use the gathering to hopefully learn new clues and info about Eleanor's death, though I doubted Caitlin would be surprised if she found out.

"I was thinking about inviting Helen from the bank," I said. "What do you think?"

"She's kind of intense," Caitlin said. "I'm not sure she'd enjoy sewing, you know, sitting still that long. I see her all the time out behind the bank, on a smoke break, I think, pacing."

"What about Tristin Terry?" I asked. "Would you be okay if I invited her?"

"Sure. Why not?"

"You told me that she and Scott used to date back in high school."

Caitlin waved away my concern. "Ancient history."

I needed to make sure I had enough pillowcases for the volunteers who showed up, so I pulled the storage box from under the cutting table. Cheddar trotted over and head-butted the box, then rubbed against my ankle.

"Look at all of these pillowcases," I said, surprised to see that the box was full.

Cheddar purred.

"I didn't realize I had so many," I said.

Volunteers dropped off pillowcases, thread, bias tape, all sorts of supplies—including those shears that had caused so much controversy between Gloria and Eleanor and made me a murder suspect. Often, I was left without knowing who'd donated the supplies and, like now, without knowing who to thank.

Cheddar spun around, raced through the room, and jumped onto the windowsill. He crouched, laid back his ears, and hissed.

Zack stood outside.

CHAPTER 18

Cheddar yowled, hissed, and swiped at Zack standing outside the window on Main Street, then hopped down and raced away.

Zack watched him go, then turned to me. "Did you teach him to do that?"

"I didn't have to," I said.

"I'd better go," Caitlin said.

We left the sewing studio. Several customers were lined up at the bakery's display counter, but Jodi and Aunt Sarah seemed to have it under control, so I went outside with Caitlin.

"I'll bring my dress by sometime," she promised, and jogged across Main Street.

Zack lingered in front of the sewing studio windows. He looked awesome in his uniform; still, the pitter-pat of my heart barely registered.

He walked over. "How's it going?"

"Okay. You?"

"Good."

Apparently, Zack's heart wasn't doing a pitter-pat, either.

My concern over the number of lost wallets reported to the visitor center had been on my mind lately. This seemed like a good time to ask Zack about it since we didn't seem to have anything else to talk about.

"Does the sheriff get a lot of reports of pickpockets in town?" I asked.

He looked at me as if I'd lost my mind.

I'd gotten that from him before.

Zack hesitated, as if he was mentally straddling the fence between a friendly chat and his deputy duties, unsure of which way to go.

"How about shoplifters?" I asked.

He still didn't respond.

"You see, I was at the visitor center looking through the log of lost items—"

"I thought you were the cleaning lady."

Was there *anyone* in town who hadn't heard that ridiculous rumor?

"I'm *not* the cleaning lady," I told him.

"That's what I heard," he said, with an apologetic shrug.

"Well, it's not true," I insisted. "Got it?"

Zack raised his hands in surrender. "Got it."

"So, are there?" I asked. "Pickpockets and shoplifters in town?"

"Why are you asking?"

He didn't seem to notice or appreciate that, as he'd requested, my questions had nothing to do with investigating Eleanor's death.

"I'm a concerned citizen," I told him.

Zack studied me for a few seconds, as if trying to determine if something else was going on.

"A few reports," he finally said.

"You keep it quiet so as not to discourage tourists. Right?" I said.

"The sheriff's office investigates every crime reported," he told me.

Obviously, Zack had no intention of giving me any information about possible pickpockets in town ripping off tourists, or shoplifters targeting our stores. Obvious, too, was the fact that he displayed none of the I'm-interested vibe I used to get from him, which, honestly, suited me fine.

Since things weren't going well between us, I saw no reason not to make them worse.

"You're covering for Owen, aren't you?" I said.

"Covering—"

He stopped, realizing what I was getting at, and clammed up, which answered my question.

"He's cheating on Willow, you know about it, and you're not saying anything," I said.

"I don't know what you're talking about."

"You men. You're always covering for each other. Admit it."

"I know nothing about Owen cheating."

"It's Marissa, isn't it?" I said, remembering how she'd leered at Owen through the front window of the visitor center. "He's cheating on Willow with Marissa."

Once more, Zack looked at me as if I'd lost my mind.

"I'm right, aren't I?"

Zack shifted into deputy mode, all expression disappearing from his face, giving away nothing. To me, that meant he knew something. Now I was even more convinced it was Marissa who was cheating with Owen.

Since Zack refused to confirm my suspicion, I hadn't learned anything about all the wallets lost in Hideaway Grove, or gotten any info on shoplifters in town, I didn't know what else to talk to him about. He, apparently, felt the same way.

"I've got to go," I said.

"Me too."

He didn't linger for another second, nor did I.

I pushed through the door into the bakery. I didn't look back.

Thoughts of Eleanor's murder, Owen cheating, lost wallets, and shoplifters crowded my thoughts as I worked on a new order for tote bags that the gift shop had sent. I was relieved the order wouldn't take long to fill—meaning I'd get paid pretty soon—but I didn't feel particularly happy about it. I wasn't sure why. Maybe it was the thoughts of Zack that kept creeping into my head. I hadn't been all that happy with him, either, lately, and he seemed to feel the same. I wasn't sure what, if anything, I should do about it.

With the gift shop order completed, that meant I could turn my attention to the tote bags Brooke had requested for her upcoming bachelorette party. I hadn't looked at her design yet, but, somehow, I felt that no matter what I produced she wouldn't like it. I couldn't face tackling it right now.

The only thing I knew for certain that I could handle with some degree of success was a pillowcase dress party. I pulled the box of pillowcases from under the table and sorted through them, picking out the prettiest ones to use first. Some of them were exceptional. The volunteers would love turning them into dresses.

I checked my supplies and saw that I had plenty of rickrack and lace to embellish the dresses. Bias tape in white and ivory—the colors most used—was running low, but I decided I had enough for the upcoming party. I spent a few minutes winding bobbins for each sewing machine—everybody hates to wind the bobbin—in a variety of colors so they were ready to go, too.

All I needed now were volunteers.

I sent a text message with the party details to everyone who usually helped with the project and reminded them that

Aunt Sarah's famous sugar cookies would be served, always a crowd-pleaser.

I wanted to keep the charity project open to everyone. After consulting Caitlin and getting her thoughts on inviting two new people, I decided to ask Helen and Tristin to join us. Honestly, that whole thing about Tristin and Scott dating back in high school seemed a bit weird to me, but if Caitlin was okay with it, I was, too. As for Helen, I'd never thought of the bank assistant manager as too fidgety to sit still long enough to sew a dress, but I guess Caitlin knew her better than I did.

Grabbing my things, I left the sewing studio. In the bakery, I noticed Aunt Sarah wasn't there. Jodi was at the work island in the kitchen. Something smelled awesome, reminding me of my expanding waistline. All my other pants fit okay, but my favorite jeans didn't, and I was determined to get into them . . . somehow.

"Where's Aunt Sarah?" I called.

Jodi glanced up. "She's running an errand."

I asked if she needed anything. She didn't so I left the bakery. On Main Street, I caught myself glancing around, expecting to see Zack. Annoyed with myself—and him, for some reason—I headed down the street.

Anna waved to me from the doorway of her thrift shop as I approached, looking troubled.

"I got your text about the next pillowcase dress party," she said when I stopped.

The entrance to her thrift shop was crowded with merchandise selected to lure shoppers inside. A tea cart held delicate cups and saucers, figurines of cats and roosters, and cloth napkins rolled and tied with pink ribbon. Nearby sat a wooden magazine rack and an umbrella stand shaped like an elephant's foot.

Anna was one of my pillowcase dress party regulars. I

could always count on her being there. I wondered if her frown indicated she had a conflict.

"Can you make it?" I asked.

"Oh, sure." She shook her head. "But here's the thing. I got pillowcases from Clara. You know, my cousin in Los Angeles. She gets those lovely pillowcases from the estate sales she visits. Well, I can't find them."

Anna glanced inside her store, and I did, too, as if we both might suddenly spot a stack of pillowcases sitting in plain sight.

"Did you stop by and pick them up?" she asked.

I'd done that before but not without Anna's okay.

"No," I said. "Maybe one of the other ladies sold them by mistake."

"I can't imagine they would. Everyone knows I save them for your parties." Anna's frown deepened and she shook her head. "And this batch was so nice. Clara picks out only the best."

"Maybe they'll turn up," I offered.

I'd seen Anna's stockroom. She kept it neat and well organized, but with three other ladies working there, anything could have happened.

"I have plenty on hand," I said. "More than enough for the next party."

Anna still looked troubled. "I'll bring them, if I find them."

She went back into the thrift shop, and I crossed Main Street, on to my next errand.

The Bank of Hideaway Grove looked stately and dignified but not as warm and welcoming as you might expect in a town where flower boxes and water bowls sat outside most of the businesses, and merchandise was on display.

A hush hung over the bank when I walked in, almost as if I'd entered the public library. I remembered that Anna had mentioned she'd witnessed Eleanor and Helen in something of a tiff outside in front of the drugstore. In here, in this atmosphere, even a slightly raised voice would be a major event.

The two young women who worked as tellers, safely ensconced behind barred windows, smiled pleasantly as they waited on customers. Mr. Jarvis, the bank manager, sat at his desk at the back of the room, keeping watch, as if he not only expected something untoward might happen, but actually hoped it would so he could intervene and put a stop to it.

Helen sat at her desk situated closer to the front of the room. She wore a gray business suit, accessorized with pearls, reminding me again of my job in Los Angeles. She studied her computer screen, tapped the keyboard, and shuffled papers across her desk, looking efficient and competent doing whatever it was assistant bank managers did all day.

"Hi, Helen." I approached her desk, the library vibe in the room and the stink eye I was getting from Mr. Jarvis causing me to keep my voice low.

She looked up, a standard customer-service smile on her face—which vanished immediately when she got a good look at me. Helen glanced back at Mr. Jarvis, then looked at me again. Her eyes narrowed.

"I knew you'd show up here eventually." She squeezed the words out in an angry snarl.

What the heck? Caitlin had told me Helen wasn't likely to come to my pillowcase dress party, but I hadn't expected such venom from her.

She looked back at Mr. Jarvis once more. He was on the phone.

"Well, you're here now. Let's get this over with."

Helen rose from her chair and stalked across the office, leaving me to follow. We went down a short hallway, past a small conference room, a restroom, the employee break-

room, and out the back door into the parking lot. The lot
was shared by several businesses that faced Main Street.
Only a few cars were there and fewer people.

Helen pulled a pack of cigarettes from the pocket of her
jacket and drew one out. She waved it at me.

"I know what you're thinking. I know why you're here."
Some of the anger was gone from her voice, replaced by
worry and fear.

I had no idea what she was talking about but figured it had
nothing to do with my pillowcase dress parties.

"But I didn't—I did not—kill Eleanor Franklin," she told
me. "I know you've been asking around, trying to find out
what happened to her. But I didn't kill her. I don't care what
you saw."

Stunned, I couldn't say anything.

"I was there. Yes. I was there. I admit it." Helen held the
cigarette between her fingers.

My thoughts shuffled fast, trying to keep up with what
she was saying.

"You were at the government center the morning Eleanor
was murdered," I realized.

"I know you saw me there."

Actually, I didn't. In fact, I'd racked my brain trying to
recall who might have been there that morning that I recognized, and I'd come up with no one.

"I saw you looking around before you went inside."
Helen touched the unlit cigarette to her lips. "I'm surprised
Sheriff Grumman hasn't come here questioning me yet."

"I haven't told the sheriff anything," I said, which was
true. And if I'd seen Helen there that morning, I wouldn't
have implicated her by mentioning it to him—not until I'd
found out for myself why she was there.

She looked surprised. "Well, thank you for not dragging
me into the investigation. That's all I need."

"The sheriff still might want to question you," I said.

"I've heard talk around town that you and Eleanor had a confrontation. He's probably heard it, too."

Startled, Helen said, "All right, all right. That happened. Eleanor and I didn't get along. Everybody knew it. It's no secret. But it was Eleanor's fault. She started it. Sticking her nose in where it didn't belong."

"What was it about?" I asked.

"Nothing," Helen insisted, though from her tone I knew it was actually something. "Eleanor put herself in the middle of a situation that didn't concern her, as usual. I'd addressed it with Gloria. It was handled."

I'd heard from someone that they'd witnessed a tense moment between Helen and Gloria.

"What happened with Gloria?" I asked.

"It was banking business. Confidential. I can't discuss it."

I understood her need to keep the details quiet. But she was a witness at the scene of Eleanor's murder. I couldn't let this opportunity pass.

"Who else did you see that morning at the government center?" I asked.

"Lots of people. You know how busy those offices can get, especially in the morning."

"Anybody going into or out of the visitor center?" I asked.

Helen pressed the unlit cigarette between her lips once more, thinking.

"I didn't see anybody," she said. "But I was only watching for a few minutes. I had to . . . go."

"You must have seen the sheriff at the visitor center later," I said. "Why didn't you come forward?"

"I was in a hurry. I had to get to the bank. I can't be late. This place . . ." Helen drew herself up. "Just because I had a confrontation with Eleanor, doesn't mean I killed her."

I wasn't so sure about that.

She stowed the cigarette in the pocket of her jacket and nodded toward the bank's door.

"I've got to get back in there," she said.

Helen went inside, looking like someone who was headed for her own execution. It made me think of how I'd sometimes felt about my job in Los Angeles, toward the end, especially.

Not a great memory.

Then something else hit me.

What was Helen doing at the government center that morning?

CHAPTER 19

"You're not going to believe what happened," Lily declared.

We stood on the sidewalk outside Flights of Flowers. I was headed for the visitor center; she'd rushed outside when she saw me walk past.

She'd startled me with her approach. My thoughts had been focused on my meeting with Helen outside the bank yesterday. No matter how I replayed our conversation, I was convinced Helen belonged on my mental list of suspects.

She'd admitted being near the scene of Eleanor's murder. She hadn't come forward and told Sheriff Grumman she'd been there. She'd admitted that she and Eleanor didn't get along. I knew that whatever had gone on between them was personal and, thus, a motive for murder, since she'd also had a confrontation with Gloria but wouldn't give details because it was a confidential bank matter.

Obviously, Helen was hiding something.

I hadn't thought to ask Helen why she was at the government center so early that morning and not at the bank, but why else would she have been there on that particular day, at that particular time, except to murder Eleanor?

For a few moments last night when I'd been tossing and turning, my brain full of suspects, I'd considered reporting Helen's presence close to the crime scene to Sheriff Grumman in the hope he might have knowledge I wasn't aware of that would link Helen to the murder. He would, of course, question her. She'd, of course, report seeing me there. Even though the sheriff already knew I was there, no way did I want to give him another reminder, so I decided to keep it to myself—for now.

"Have you heard of it?" Lily asked.

I snapped back to the moment, realizing she'd been telling me something and, once again, my thoughts had been consumed by Eleanor's murder.

Lily went on, thankfully. "It's Hero's Bar and Grill, but it's mostly a bar. Over in Holden."

"I haven't heard of it."

"Everybody says it is a really cool place and the woman who owns it is a hoot," Lily said. "It's kind of a getaway for people in Hideaway Grove who want to go someplace different."

I wasn't sure where this conversation was going.

"So, Willow told Owen she wanted them to go, and he refused," Lily said. "Flat refused."

Now I got it.

"You think that's where Owen is meeting the new girlfriend," I said.

I didn't want to tell Lily that I suspected Marissa was the new girlfriend, not until I knew for sure.

"What else could it be?" Lily huffed. "Why else would he refuse to take Willow there?"

"Makes sense."

"Here's what I'm thinking. The next time Owen breaks a date with Willow, you should go straight to Hero's," Lily told me. "You can see if he's there and, you know, catch him in the act."

"Wouldn't you rather confront him?"

"No." Lily shook her head. "If I walked in and saw him there with someone else, I would lose my mind, and it would get really ugly—even for a bar."

Lily was petite with a cute blond ponytail. It was hard to imagine her starting a bar fight. But where a cheating boyfriend was concerned, anything could happen.

"I'll check it out," I said. "Just let me know when Owen breaks another date."

"You bet I will."

Lily marched back into the flower shop, and I headed for the visitor center.

Marissa sat at her usual desk when I walked in, slouched in the chair, and focused on her phone. So far, I hadn't seen her perform one single function for the visitor center.

Apparently, I'm the only one who noticed.

"Morning," I said, as I sat at the desk beside hers, and stowed my tote in the bottom drawer.

Marissa didn't respond.

"Where's Harriet?" I asked.

She said nothing.

"Marissa? Where's—"

"Meeting with the mayor," she said, not looking up from her phone.

"About what?"

"Beats me."

Dealing with Marissa seemed more of a trial than usual this morning. I decided to switch to another topic, maybe find out if she was really involved with Owen.

"Have you heard about a place in Holden? Hero's Bar and Grill?" I asked.

"Everybody's heard of that place," she responded, as if I was a total moron for asking.

"Have you been?"

"Everybody's been."

Maybe I need to work on my interrogation skills.

I left my desk and walked over to her.

"When were you there?" I asked, trying to sound casual.

The front door swung open, and Gloria breezed into the visitor center. Her hair, makeup, and nails were done. She had on a royal-blue skirt and jacket with matching shoes, and she carried a—oh my, I was pretty sure that was a Gucci handbag.

"Well, would you look at who showed up this morning," Marissa murmured.

"Good morning, good morning," Gloria called, a bright smile on her face as she crossed the room.

"I'm surprised to see her here, after yesterday," Marissa mumbled.

Gloria dropped her handbag on the desk she always used, then disappeared through the door into the storage room, no hesitation. Seemed that being at the scene of Eleanor's death still didn't bother her.

"What happened yesterday?" I asked Marissa.

"Living it up pretty good," she said.

At Hero's Bar and Grill? I wondered.

"My grandma saw her," Marissa said. "She sees her a lot."

Maybe there was a senior day at the bar.

"In Elliot," Marissa said, seeing the confused look on my face. "At the casino."

I knew there was a casino in Elliot, a town less than an hour's drive from Hideaway Grove, but I didn't know anyone who'd been—and I sure didn't expect it would be Gloria.

"They have a bingo hall. Grandma goes. She sees lots of people from town in there, you know, playing the slots, whatever," Marissa said. "Not exactly a high-rolling day for Gloria yesterday, but she didn't seem to mind. That's what my grandma told me."

The door to the storage room opened and Gloria walked in, carrying a cup of coffee. She grabbed the luxe log from the top of the filing cabinet and sat down at her desk. She opened the log, got out her cell phone and swiped screens, and sipped her coffee.

I gave her a few minutes to get settled, then walked over.

"I wanted to talk to you about Lois Atwater's lost wallet," I said.

"I know about her wallet," Gloria told me, not bothering to look at me. "It was returned to her. It's handled."

"Well, no, not really," I said.

Gloria sipped her coffee. "That certainly has nothing to do with me."

"Actually, it does," I pointed out.

"No, it doesn't," she insisted. "I shipped it to her. That's all I can do."

"She received a wallet, but it isn't hers," I said. "There was a mix-up in the shipping."

"There was no mix-up." Gloria finally looked up at me, angry. "I returned her wallet to her."

"But she said—"

"Obviously, she's confused." Gloria's voice rose. "The woman couldn't keep up with her wallet when she was here—it's no wonder she doesn't recognize it when it's shipped to her."

Gloria's attitude surprised me and was starting to irk me a bit.

"Lois was very clear," I said, forcing myself to remain calm. "Her wallet was very special to her—"

"I've been keeping track of the luxury items for a long time, and I assure you this sort of thing happens all the time," Gloria told me, her anger growing. "Tourists claim they haven't received their item back. They don't realize the package has arrived. It's lying outside their house, where the delivery person tossed it. Another family member brought it inside and didn't mention it. Their neighbor stole it. It gets delivered to the wrong address. This is all quite normal."

I drew a breath. "But this isn't a delivery problem, it's a—"

Gloria slammed the luxe log closed and pushed to her feet.

"If you think you should involve yourself in something I've been handling perfectly well for a long time, then talk to Harriet about it."

Gloria grabbed her handbag and stormed out of the visitor center.

Stunned, Marissa and I both stared at each other in the silence.

"I guess losing all that money yesterday made her pretty grumpy after all," Marissa said.

"I guess so," I said.

Gloria was territorial about her responsibilities here. I'd seen that sort of thing before, and I understood it. Yet I couldn't help thinking her reaction was a bit out of proportion to the situation.

"Are you going to talk to Harriet about taking over the luxe items?" Marissa asked.

It would be a wasted effort, I knew. Harriet would take Gloria's side to avoid a confrontation, and the whole thing would leave Harriet upset; I didn't want to be the cause of any more stress in her life. Still, I wanted Lois to have her wallet back.

"I'll figure out something," I said.

When my shift ended, I went to the bakery. Jodi waved as she waited on a mom with two little girls at the display case. Aunt Sarah stood in the kitchen frowning at her cell phone.

"Something wrong?" I asked.

Aunt Sarah looked up. "Just working out next month's budget."

"Anything I can do to help?"

She smiled. "It's under control."

The bell over the front door chimed and Caitlin walked in.

"I can't come to the party tonight. I have to help get Dad to his doctor's appointment," she said. "But I thought you could use some help getting ready for the party."

We went into the sewing studio. I opened both windows—they glided effortlessly—and we got busy setting up for the volunteers. So far, I'd heard from three people, but others might let me know later, or simply show up.

The volunteers liked to pick out the pillowcase they wanted to sew, so I spread the ones I'd selected earlier across the cutting table.

"I thought you'd bring your wedding dress," I said.

Caitlin froze as she placed scissors at each of the sewing machines set up on the banquet tables.

"Oh. I forgot."

She forgot? Brides usually wouldn't miss an opportunity to show off their wedding dress.

"Are you sure you're okay with the wedding?" I asked.

"Of course." Caitlin gave herself a little shake. "I'm just distracted, that's all. You know, with the store, Dad, Mom, and . . . everything."

Her reasoning made sense but, still, something didn't seem quite right.

"I'm here for you," I said. "If you need anything, or if you just want to talk about . . . anything."

Caitlin gave me a quick smile. "Thanks, but I'm fine."

We readied the sewing studio for tonight, sweeping the floor, distributing the thread, notions, and trims between the sewing machines. Cheddar hopped up into the windowsill and watched us for a few minutes, then took off again.

"I guess that's it," I said, as I put the broom away.

"Sugar cookies tonight, I hope."

"Of course."

When we went into the bakery I spotted Lily at the display case, then realized, no, it was Willow. The sisters looked a lot alike, both petite with blond hair. Willow had on pastel scrubs, reminding me that she worked in a doctor's office.

I'd agreed to find out if Owen was cheating on Willow. Something else that had seemed like a good idea at the time. Now I felt kind of icky seeing her, knowing what I knew. Plus, I was annoyed with Owen for possibly cheating on Willow, Marissa for possibly cheating with Owen, and Zack because he'd refused to come clean and tell me the truth about who was cheating with whom—or not.

Mostly, I was annoyed with myself for not resolving the matter already.

"Congrats on your upcoming wedding," Willow said to Caitlin when we joined her at the display counter. "How exciting!"

"Thanks," Caitlin said.

"And the bridal show is coming up," Willow went on. "You must be really anxious to see everything."

"Well . . . sure."

"Who wouldn't be?" Willow glanced at Caitlin's hand and frowned. "Where's your ring?"

"Oh. That." Caitlin covered her left hand with her right. "I, uh, I don't wear it when I'm working."

A dreamy look came over Willow's face and she lowered her voice a little.

"Owen and I have looked at engagement rings," she said.

"He proposed?" Caitlin asked, surprised.

"Not yet," she said. "But I'm hoping."

Now I felt even ickier.

"We were just walking by the jewelry store and stopped to look in the display window. We've done that a couple of times. One of the rings stole my heart. It was gorgeous." Willow paused, as if reality suddenly set in. "I know I can't expect much—you know how it is on a deputy's salary. But I'll be thrilled with whatever—if it happens, of course."

I no longer felt icky. Now I felt yucky.

"Here you go," Jodi said as she approached the display case with a pink bakery box.

Willow left the bakery and Caitlin and I moved along with her, then all of us stopped quickly when we nearly collided with Tristin Terry on the sidewalk. Her gaze hopped from one to another of us, and she took a step back.

"Did you get my text?" I asked. "About the pillowcase party tonight?"

"Uh . . . yeah." Tristin shifted uncomfortably.

"I hope you can come," I said.

"Maybe." She gulped and looked away. "I've got to go." Tristin hurried away.

I didn't know her well, but her conduct seemed odd. I wondered if she didn't like me, for some reason. Or maybe it was—Willow.

Was that uncomfortable look on Tristin's face because she'd encountered Willow?

Was Tristin the one cheating with Owen?

CHAPTER 20

"My favorite." Anna headed for the tray of sugar cookies I'd set up, along with bottles of water, on the end of one of the sewing tables. She popped a cookie into her mouth and took another. "Nobody makes a sugar cookie like Sarah."

"I'll say." Connie, who'd come into the sewing studio on Anna's heels, helped herself to a cookie.

Connie and Anna had both confirmed my invitation to tonight's pillowcase dress party. I'd invited Tristin, too, but after our awkward meeting outside the bakery, I doubted she'd show up. Valerie had arrived minutes earlier and was now looking at the pillowcases I'd spread out on the cutting table.

"Did Harriet give you the go-ahead to make the vests?" Connie asked.

I'd scheduled tonight's pillowcase dress party in the hope that the ladies could provide a clue, a lead, a witness, *something* that would help me find Eleanor's killer. I didn't expect the opportunity to ease her murder investigation into the conversation to present itself so early in the evening, but I went with it.

"I haven't talked to her about the vests yet," I said. "Things have been kind of tense at the visitor center lately."

"There's tension all over town," Valerie declared.

"It would help if the sheriff could solve Eleanor's murder," I said.

"Lost and Found Day is postponed," Valerie went on. "The dish ladies postponed, too."

"And rent going up," Anna said, around a mouthful of cookie.

Connie shook her head. "I can't believe Gloria is doing that."

I wanted us to talk about Eleanor's death. How had Gloria gotten into the conversation?

"Doing what?" I asked.

"Didn't you know?" Connie asked. "Gloria's the one behind the rent increases. She owns property all over Hideaway Grove."

True, I didn't know Gloria all that well, but I hadn't pictured her as a landlord.

"Gloria and her husband," Valerie pointed out. "Reggie was smart with money, and extremely conservative. Now, of course, with him gone Gloria owns all those properties, and she's increasing the rent significantly on every one of them."

"Reggie never would have done that," Connie said. "He was the nicest guy. He understood what people were dealing with financially. He knew how tough it was to make ends meet."

"I heard that Eleanor left her house to Rayna," I said. "Eleanor's death couldn't have happened at a better time."

"That Gloria. She's certainly showed her true self since Reggie died," Anna said.

"Her conduct is despicable—on many levels," Valerie declared.

Valerie shared a meaningful look with Connie and Anna.

"Amen to that," Connie said.

Anna swiped another cookie and nodded.

I tried again.

"I heard that Helen at the bank had some sort of argument with Eleanor," I said. "Seems they didn't like each other."

Anna gulped down another cookie. "I heard that Gloria's sister-in-law had visited Mr. Schwartz."

"Isn't he the nicest man?" Valerie said.

"Everybody thinks the world of him," Connie agreed.

"Why was Wanda consulting with him?" Valerie asked.

"There's some sort of problem with Gloria's husband's will," Anna said. "I heard that Wanda suspected Gloria had changed Reggie's will, then forged his signature, cutting out Wanda's two sons."

How did we get back on Gloria?

"Something is definitely up," Valerie said. "Gloria is shopping like a madwoman, spending money like crazy."

"Everywhere but in Hideaway Grove," Connie said.

"Has anyone heard anything about the sheriff's investigation?" I asked.

"I see Gloria drive by almost every day, headed for the freeway," Anna said. "She's going somewhere quite frequently."

"Probably buying all those expensive clothes and accessories she's been wearing around town," Valerie said.

"Spending Reggie's insurance money on that?" Connie shook her head. "How foolish."

"So, about Eleanor's death," I said. "Have any of you—"

"Oh, my goodness! Would you just look!" Anna rushed to the cutting table and gestured to the pillowcases I'd laid out. "These are mine. The ones Clara got for me from the estate sales."

Everyone turned to Anna and the pillowcases, and the surprised look on her face.

"How on earth did they get here?" Anna exclaimed.

"They were in my storage box," I explained.

"No." Anna shook her head. "These are the ones I mentioned to you. The special ones Clara had found. I was holding them in my stockroom, waiting for the next party. Then they . . . disappeared."

"Are you sure you didn't drop them off?" Connie asked.

Anna frowned. "Well, I didn't think I had, but . . ."

"They certainly are lovely," Valerie said. "Let's get started, shall we?"

The ladies spent a few minutes deciding which pillowcase they wanted to work on tonight, then gave it to me. I sized each pillowcase, cut the armholes, and handed them back. Everyone clustered at the end of the table to work on the casings for each dress.

"Seeing you use those shears makes me think of Eleanor," Valerie said, as she pinned the casing in place.

Finally, we could talk about Eleanor's murder investigation.

"Such a thoughtful donation," Connie agreed. "That was Eleanor, always helpful, always volunteering."

"I've never known anyone more concerned about the future of Hideaway Grove," Valerie said. "She was worried about the rents going up in town and encouraged renters not to pay the increase."

Somehow, I'd lost total control of my murder investigation.

"I heard," Valerie went on, "that Eleanor was the one who encouraged Wanda to consult with Mr. Schwartz about Reggie's will."

No one was picking up on my hints. Time to be more direct.

"Can you think of anyone who would want to hurt Eleanor?" I asked.

"Eleanor was so friendly," Anna mused. "I used to see her chatting with her neighbor all the time."

Good grief.

"Which neighbor was that?" Valerie asked.

"Mona. Right next door. In the blue house," Anna said.

"Oh yes, Mona." Valerie nodded. "She's had her share of troubles."

"Once, I saw Eleanor doing her yard work for her," Anna said.

"Eleanor was a dear." Valerie sighed. "I'll think of her every time I'm here and use those scissors she donated."

"And try to forget the stink Gloria made over them," Connie added.

Here we were, back to Gloria again.

"So, about Eleanor's death," I said.

"I'm so sorry, Abbey," Anna said. "I can't talk about Eleanor. The whole thing is just too sad."

"It is," Valerie agreed.

Connie held up her pillowcase. "I think I'll trim this with some lace. Pink, and plenty of it."

"Adorable," Anna declared.

The ladies moved to the sewing tables. I'd arranged the two tables so they faced each other, making it easy for us to chat while we sewed. The ladies sat down behind their usual sewing machine and got busy.

I stood at the cutting table, holding the shears, watching them. This wasn't exactly how I'd hoped the evening would turn out. I needed to solve Eleanor's murder and I'd really hoped the ladies could provide some new info, but I hadn't gotten any answers. Instead, I'd been left with a major question.

A lot of people didn't like Gloria, and she was still alive.

A lot of people did like Eleanor, and she was murdered.

What was I missing?

*   *   *

Maybe I had too many suspects. Maybe I had the wrong suspects. Maybe I should forget everything I'd discovered so far—little though it was—and start over.

Starting over wasn't a bad idea, especially after last night.

Main Street was coming to life as I walked through town. Merchants were sweeping the sidewalk, setting out signs announcing the day's sales, and displaying featured stock. Life, as usual, in Hideaway Grove—except that a murderer was among us.

None of the ladies at last night's pillowcase dress party had added anything to my investigation. No new clues, no new suspects, no motive. Yet, someone, somewhere, didn't like Eleanor—why else would she have been murdered?

I was missing something, something important, something crucial to the investigation. I couldn't put my finger on it. But it was there, somewhere. It had to be. I had to try harder, think a different way, reach out in a new direction—I had to.

Still, Sheriff Grumman hadn't been able to solve the crime, so maybe I shouldn't be so hard on myself, I thought. However, I had more at stake. I couldn't have the sheriff's suspicion that I'd murdered Eleanor hanging over my head forever.

Up ahead I saw the visitor center, my destination for this morning. Things had been so slow there lately, I figured it wouldn't matter if I wasn't there exactly on time. In fact, I doubted anyone would notice.

Even though the ladies at the pillowcase dress party last night hadn't provided me with a clear path to Eleanor's killer, they'd given me two new people to question. Both of them had been recipients of Eleanor's goodwill and kindness. It seemed unlikely they could point out her murderer, but it was all I had to go on at the moment.

I left Main Street and headed down Blue Bird Lane. Anna had mentioned that she'd seen Eleanor chatting with Mona, her neighbor, quite often. I hoped she could provide some new info.

When I reached the end of the block, I knew right away which house belonged to Eleanor. Rayna had told me it was situated behind the place she rented on Dove Drive, but even without that knowledge, I could have picked it out.

Eleanor's home displayed everything expected of a home-owner in Hideaway Grove. Painted mint green, it had a pristine white picket fence, a perfectly manicured lawn, carefully tended shrubs, and beds of blooming flowers. A colorful wreath hung on the front door and sculpted topiaries sat on the porch.

Beside it, the blue house Anna had mentioned that belonged to Mona hadn't received the same attention. By no means was it an eyesore, but the lawn was slightly over-grown, and the flower beds needed weeding. No wreath hung on the front door. Seemed Mona was having trouble keeping up the place; she must have really appreciated Eleanor helping out with the yard work.

The gate squeaked when I opened it and walked up the sidewalk to the porch. I figured I wouldn't have to ask Mona anything, really. She'd been neighbors with Eleanor for quite a while, so I knew she'd be anxious to share the good times they'd had. It might be a challenge to direct our conversation to Eleanor's murder. I'd have to be subtle and use some finesse to get the information I needed.

Voices sounded inside the house—the TV, I thought—as I rang the doorbell. After a few seconds, the drapes that covered the front window parted slightly, a woman peeked out, and the drapes were yanked closed again.

Footsteps approached the door.

"Come back with a warrant!"

Stunned, I stood there for a few seconds. What the heck was going on?

"Hello?" I called through the closed door. "I'm not the police."

Silence from inside the house.

"I'm Abbey Chandler," I said. "I work at the visitor center."

The door jerked open and a woman glared at me. She looked fortyish, tall, thin, no makeup, her hair hanging loose around her shoulders, dressed in faded jeans and a somewhat unflattering T-shirt.

"Mona?" I asked.

"Yeah, that's me," she barked. "You're from the visitor center, huh? You're the one. I applied for a job on the cleaning crew at the government center and they gave it to you instead."

Would that rumor ever die?

"No, that's wrong," I said.

"If you're not the cleaning lady, why are you here?" she demanded. Her eyes widened. "You're from the mayor's office, aren't you? You're one of those so-called cultural inspectors."

I'd never heard of a cultural inspector.

"I'm here about Eleanor—"

"Oh, great. That's just great." Mona flung out both arms, then let them slap against her sides. "Eleanor's dead and still she won't leave me alone."

Obviously, I wasn't going to need much subtlety or finesse to get info out of Mona.

"The sheriff, he came around, too. Asking questions. Carrying on like I had something to do with Eleanor getting herself killed," Mona said, her anger growing. "I swear, you make one little mistake, and it follows you forever."

Sheriff Grumman had questioned Mona? Did that mean he considered her a suspect?

"Well, this time I was justified." Mona's anger kept building. "That Eleanor, she threatened me. Over and over. Christmas, Easter, Halloween—Flag Day, for goodness' sake. Flag Day!"

I took a step back.

No way had I expected this response from Mona. All I knew to do was keep going, try to learn something useful—and maybe make some sense out of what Mona was saying.

"Threatened you how?" I asked. "What did Eleanor do?"

"Constant complaints. My flowers needed to be weeded. My lawn should be mowed. Why wasn't I decorating for the holidays? I should have a wreath. Why didn't I have a wreath? Where was the wreath for my front door?" Mona drew a breath, calming slightly. "I had that little incident in the past, okay? I lost my job, okay? I haven't found a new one, okay? It's all I can do to pay the mortgage and utilities on this place, okay? And here comes Eleanor, sticking her nose in, telling me I need to fix up the place—so it will look good for the tourists."

I didn't know what to say to that.

Mona didn't give me a chance anyway.

Her anger ramped up again.

"Once, she had the nerve—the nerve—to come over here and do the yardwork herself." Mona fumed. "I told her she'd better never come back over here. I'd had enough. I told her that if she ever showed her face here again or stepped one foot into my yard, she'd be sorry."

I was kind of sorry I'd come.

"Eleanor threatened she'd turn me in to the mayor's office for not keeping my front yard up to the town's standards," Mona told me.

The mayor's office had what amounted to lawn police? I had no idea.

"Threatened me," Mona said again. "Threatened to turn me in, cause me to have to pay a fine. Plus, deal with the gossip. You know how people talk in this town, you know what it's like."

Me working as the cleaning lady at the visitor center had started somehow and continued to spread.

"Nobody else complained, just Eleanor," Mona declared. "She should have minded her own business."

"You must be relieved Eleanor is dead," I said.

"Relieved? No. More like—glad."

Mona slammed the door in my face.

Glad, huh? Glad enough to have murdered her?

Maybe.

CHAPTER 21

Mona had surprised me. I'd expected to hear yet another glowing report on how awesome Eleanor was. Instead, I'd gotten the opposite. She'd told me about another side of Eleanor I hadn't heard of before. Mona was the first person who'd come straight out and said she didn't like Eleanor. Enough to murder her?

I wondered once more why, exactly, Sheriff Grumman had questioned Mona about Eleanor's death. He must have had a reason. Something that related to the *incident* from her past that Mona had mentioned?

It seemed likely. A squabble over the upkeep of a neighbor's front yard hardly seemed like a motive for murder, I thought as I left Blue Bird Lane and headed for the visitor center. But if you add to it the mayor's office getting involved, a fine to pay, and somehow coming up with the money to have the landscaping upgraded to the town's standards, on top of dealing with the gossip, well, I guess anything could happen.

Especially where Mona was concerned. She was kind of

high strung, stressed, unemployed, struggling to get by. Obviously, she'd had all she could take of Eleanor and her good intentions.

I'd found one person who didn't like Eleanor. There were probably more, and one of them was her killer.

When I walked into the visitor center, Harriet was on the phone and Marissa sat at her desk, apparently texting someone.

"Some guy came by asking for you," Marissa mentioned without taking her eyes off her phone.

My only thought was that it must have been Mitch, wanting to update me on the window screens he was buying for the sewing studio.

"He was hot," Marissa said. "Really hot."

"Probably Mitch," I said.

"I know Mitch. He's one fine-looking man, but it wasn't him," she said. "Looked like this guy had money. And he definitely was not from around here."

I was stumped.

"What was his name?" I asked.

"Didn't say. Said he'd find you," she said. "When he does, ask him if he's got a brother, okay?"

Harriet hung up the phone, lurched out of her chair, and swung around to face us.

"We're being sued!" she shouted.

I shot to my feet, expecting her to collapse as she'd nearly done before. But instead of looking pale and overwhelmed, Harriet's cheeks flamed, and her nose flared.

"That was the daughter of one of our tourists!" Harriet pointed to the phone on her desk. "She's suing us!"

Stunned, I couldn't even ask her a question.

She didn't give me the chance anyway.

Harriet pointed to the desk Gloria always used.

"Gloria isn't here today! She's too upset to come to work!"

Harriet was absolutely furious. I'd never seen her like this before.

She swung her arm around and pointed at me.

"You involved yourself in the return of that wallet from Lois Atwater. Involved yourself when you knew Gloria handled the luxury items." Harriet pointed to the phone again. "And now we're being sued!"

I was completely lost.

"That was Lois's daughter," Harriet shouted. "She's an attorney—an attorney! She's insisting the wallet that was returned to her mother wasn't her mother's wallet."

"I know. I told Gloria that."

"It's not even a designer wallet—it's a knockoff! She's accusing us of fraud, theft, emotional distress—and who knows what else she'll come up with!"

"I see why you're upset, but—"

"Gloria told me you involved yourself with the luxe items, Abbey, without being asked to do so, without provocation," Harriet said, still seething. "She suggested you secretly involved yourself with shipping Lois's wallet, you caused this problem, and you were attempting to blame everything on Gloria."

"What?" Now I was outraged.

"To cover yourself for interfering, you contacted other tourists who'd claimed to have lost a wallet while in town, to bolster your claim that Gloria was at fault!"

"That's not true," I insisted.

"We're facing a huge lawsuit and a public relations nightmare, because of you. I have to go discuss this with the mayor and, frankly, I don't know whether you'll be working here any longer, or not."

Harried yanked her handbag off the desk and stormed out of the visitor center.

I stared after her, too stunned to say anything. How had a

mix-up in shipping turned into this major issue? How had I gotten the blame for it?

None of this would have happened if Gloria hadn't come up with that ridiculous log that nobody else could understand, and hadn't been so secretive about the contents of the luxe cabinet.

None of this was my fault. I wasn't going to take the blame for it. I had to get to the bottom of it, clear my name. Otherwise, I really might end up working as a cleaning lady somewhere.

Working at the visitor center had—like so many other things—seemed like a good idea at the time. Somehow, it had turned into a nightmare.

I sat at my desk trying to stay busy, trying not to dwell on Gloria's accusations and Harriet's threats. Harriet never returned from the mayor's office, and Marissa never spoke to me—probably for the best. Finally, my shift ended. I grabbed my things and left.

I headed down Main Street, wishing there was someone I could talk to. The image of Zack bloomed in my mind, and I melted a little. He had those wide shoulders and strong arms that would wrap me in a comforting hug, and that calming voice I'd heard a few times that always assured me everything would be all right.

Nice. Really nice.

But not likely to happen.

I pushed the image from my thoughts—and the feelings that threatened to overwhelm me—and picked up my pace.

At the bakery, I walked inside just as Jodi was placing a tray of chocolate chip cookies in the display case.

"You're just in time," she told me. "Fresh out of the oven."

She placed two cookies on a napkin and slid them toward me. They were warm, thick, filled with gooey chocolate chips.

Heck with my favorite jeans.

I grabbed both of them.

"Where's Aunt Sarah?" I asked.

"Taking care of some business," Jodi said.

I bit into one of the cookies and almost swooned, but managed to ask, "Is everything okay?"

"As far as I know," she said. "You know your aunt, she handles everything that comes along with little complaint or explanation."

Aunt Sarah had run the bakery for decades by herself; she seldom asked anyone for help.

"A gorgeous, totally hot, handsome man came by earlier looking for you," Jodi told me.

Darn it. I put the other cookie back.

"Who?" I asked.

"He didn't say," Jodi told me.

He must have been the man who'd showed up asking about me at the visitor center—which I'd forgotten about after everything that had happened this morning. I still had no idea who he could be.

I nibbled on the cookie, trying to make it last.

"What did he look like?" I asked.

"Tall, dark hair, gorgeous blue eyes." Jodi sighed. "Handsome. Enough to make my heart race."

That really wasn't much help.

"I don't think he was from around here." Jodi gave me a sly smile. "So, who is he? An old lover? Someone whose heart has ached for you? Pined away for you? Is there a man like that in your past?"

"Not that I recall."

"And now he's tracked you down." Jodi sighed dreamily. "He's come all this way, all the way to Hideaway Grove, to find you, to profess his love, to beg you to let him into your life."

"I think you're getting a little carried away."

"Maybe." Jodi giggled. "But it's fun to think about."

Yes, it was.

"He said he'd come back later," Jodi said. "And when he does, you have to promise to tell me who he is and what's going on."

"Sure."

"Now for the bad news."

I wasn't sure I could take any more bad news today.

"Sheriff Grumman was here again," Jodi said.

That's the second time he'd been here looking for me. How did he think he was going to find Eleanor's murderer when he couldn't seem to find *me*?

"I don't suppose he told you he'd found Eleanor's killer, did he?" I asked.

"I'm afraid not. He wants to talk to you again." Jodi's eyes lit up. "Maybe your mystery man will whisk you off, away from all your problems and troubles."

Actually, that sounded like a good idea.

The phone rang and Jodi disappeared into the kitchen.

I savored the last of the cookie as I went into the sewing studio, and licked the chocolate off my fingers as I opened both of the windows. Across Main Street, I spotted Caitlin coming out of the pet store carrying a garment bag, headed my way.

My spirits lifted. Just what I needed. My best friend, and a major distraction from my own problems.

I opened the pocket doors and a moment later she came into the bakery.

"Your wedding dress!" I exclaimed. "You brought it!"

"I promised I would," she said.

She came into the sewing studio. The garment bag was floor length, so we spent a few minutes raising the bar on the rack that displayed the pillowcase dresses. Caitlin hung it up, then unzipped the bag and pulled it off.

"It's gorgeous!" I said.

The gown was pale ivory silk taffeta with a sweetheart bodice topped with lace, quarter-length sleeves and a ball-gown skirt, accented with tiny pearls, beads, and crystals.

"Mom picked it out," Caitlin said. "She loves it. She said it was exactly the dress she always dreamed her daughter would wear at her wedding."

Cheddar jumped onto the windowsill, tilted his head, saw us, and yowled.

"I love the crystals," I said.

"Mom liked that, too."

Cheddar leaped off the windowsill, crouched in front of the wedding dress, and hissed.

Caitlin grinned. "I guess he's not a big fan of crystals."

Cheddar hissed again and swiped at the dress.

"No, no," I said, and tried to shoo him away.

Caitlin grabbed the skirt of the dress and pulled it out of Cheddar's reach.

Cheddar swiped at it again.

"I'm not sure about the length," Caitlin said. "Okay if I leave it here? I'll come by when I have a chance and try it on, see what you think."

"Hey, Abbey," a voice called.

I froze for an instant, knowing who'd called my name. I turned and saw Mitch standing just inside the doorway of the sewing studio.

"I wanted to let you know," he said. "I had to special order the screens for the windows—"

He spotted Caitlin and he seemed to light up.

Cheddar trotted over and wound between Mitch's ankles.

Mitch's gaze shifted to the wedding dress, then to Caitlin again. The light in his eyes faded. His shoulders slumped. He looked at her with an ache of longing so profound my heart hurt for him.

Their gazes locked, as if some unseen force bound them together. Neither spoke. Neither moved.

Mitch spun around and left the sewing studio.

Cheddar hissed at the wedding dress again, then shot across the room and leaped out the window.

Caitlin burst into tears.

CHAPTER 22

I pulled out a chair from in front of one of the sewing machines and guided Caitlin, still sobbing, to it.

"Sit down," I said.

She sat. I didn't have any tissues, so I grabbed the last of the napkins left over from my pillowcase dress party, pressed them into her hand, then pulled up a chair and sat next to her.

"I don't know why I'm crying," she managed to say.

"You've been under a lot of stress lately. Your dad's health scare, taking over the store, getting ready for your wedding."

I gestured to her wedding dress. She glanced at it and cried harder.

I didn't know what to say. All along, I'd questioned whether Caitlin was truly committed to marrying Scott. I'd never picked up on a madly-in-love vibe between them. But who was I to judge? Comment? Perhaps sway her? It wasn't my place to interfere. I didn't want to feel responsible for whatever might happen between them if I spoke up. Still . . .

Caitlin calmed down a bit. "It's just pre-wedding jitters, right?"

"Well . . ."

"That's all it is, isn't it?"

"Well . . ."

"Abbey, you're my best friend. You have to tell me the truth."

"Well . . ."

Caitlin worried the soggy napkin between her fingers, not waiting for my response.

"My parents have spent money for the wedding," she said. "They're excited. Scott's parents are thrilled. They're all making plans for how great life will be when Scott and I get married."

I tried to think of something positive to say, then came up with, "It's good you have everyone's support."

It sounded kind of lame but, luckily, she wasn't paying much attention.

"Dad needs to retire—he has to. His health is getting worse. But he won't abandon the store to just anyone. Mom's had it with always being tied to Hideaway Grove because of the store. She wants to travel," Caitlin said. "But none of that can happen until I take over the store. And then . . . then . . ."

"You'll be the one tied to Hideaway Grove."

"Yes." Caitlin sniffed. "I used to envy you. Back when we were young, and your parents moved to England and took you to different places all around the world."

I remembered those days. I'd rather have been in Hideaway Grove.

"It seemed so exciting," Caitlin said. "Just pick up and go somewhere new."

Lately, I've felt that way myself.

"I've hardly been anywhere or done anything." Tears rolled down Caitlin's cheeks again. "That sounds selfish, doesn't it? It does. How can I be that selfish? How can I do that to my parents?"

"It's okay to think about yourself, too," I pointed out.

She wiped her tears. "Scott and I . . . we've known each other all our lives. We get along fine. It's like everybody always knew we'd end up together. Like it was preordained. Like his family and my family would one day unite and form this power family."

"That's a lot of pressure on you two," I said. "How does Scott feel?"

She shrugged. "I don't know. We haven't talked about it."

That certainly didn't bode well for a marriage.

I'd tried to stay neutral and just listen. But I couldn't hold back on the one question I'd always had about Caitlin's engagement to Scott.

"Do you love him?" I asked.

She looked up at me, seeming lost for a moment.

"Yes . . . I guess."

"You don't know for sure?" I asked.

"I don't know anything right now." Caitlin burst into tears again.

I slid my arm around her shoulders and gave her a hug, then hung on for another minute until she calmed down again.

Despite my efforts, I'd done a poor job of avoiding involving myself in her decision. No need to stop now.

"Does Mitch figure into this somewhere?" I asked.

"No—yes." Caitlin drew a ragged breath. "I've tried not to have feelings for him. Really, I have. But . . ."

"You're not sure?"

"All I know for sure is that if this wedding doesn't take place, everybody will be crushed." Caitlin found some inner strength, gulped down her tears, and sat up straight. "I can't do that to Mom and Dad, or Scott's family."

It seemed her decision was made, and she was determined to live by it.

"If you want to talk again, I'm always here for you," I said.

"Thank you."

Caitlin rose, drew a determined breath, and left the sewing studio, without a glance at her wedding dress.

I wanted to talk to Mitch. After seeing that devastated look on his face when he'd been confronted with Caitlin and her wedding dress, I knew I had to check on him. Of course, I couldn't think of one thing to say that might make him feel better. Sometimes, just knowing a friend cared helped.

I hoped this was one of those times.

Heading down Hawk Avenue from Main Street, I saw that the garage door on Mitch's house was down, and his truck wasn't in the driveway. Maybe he was cruising around, listening to music, thinking things over. Or maybe he was at the Night Owl, having a beer, trying to figure out what to do. I couldn't blame him for either.

Last time I'd been here I'd gone to Kendall's house, hoping she could provide some insight into what had happened at the visitor center the morning of Eleanor's murder. She'd left town suddenly, causing me to add her name to my suspect list. I wondered now if maybe she'd returned. Since I was this close, I decided to check. Maybe I could make some progress in my investigation.

When I walked up, the house looked the same as last time I'd been here. No noticeable improvements to justify the rent increase. I rang the bell and knocked, and right away the door opened. A young woman looked out at me. She was about my age, dressed in leggings and a T-shirt, barefoot. For a couple of seconds, I thought it was Kendall, then realized I was wrong.

"Hi," I said. "I'm looking for Kendall."

"Sorry," she said with a shrug. "I just moved in a couple of days ago. Nobody here by that name."

I thanked her and left, disappointed but not surprised that Kendall hadn't returned. Seems she was gone for good, leaving me no way to mark her name off my suspect list or investigate her possible involvement any further.

Once more I thought how helpful it would be if I found someone else who'd been at the visitor center that morning.

When I got back to the street, I spotted Mitch's pickup truck swinging into his driveway. He got out and spotted me as I walked up.

One thing about talking to men, you could usually be direct. No subtlety, no finesse required.

"I know that was tough on you," I said.

He knew what I meant and didn't bother with acting as if seeing the woman he loved with her wedding gown hadn't impaled his already breaking heart.

"I decided to take that job," he said.

"For the client in France?"

Mitch nodded. "Seems like a good time to be . . . anywhere but here."

He'd decided this was the best way to handle the situation. I couldn't blame him. Hanging around Hideaway Grove, overhearing the inevitable stories about the run-up to Caitlin's wedding, living through the day the ceremony took place, knowing she and Scott were on their honeymoon, would be almost impossible to deal with.

Caitlin had told me nothing in confidence, yet sharing her doubts about the wedding wasn't right. But it was tough standing here, looking at how upset Mitch appeared, and not saying anything.

"You know, anything could happen," I said, and tried to put a little optimism into my voice.

Mitch shook his head. He didn't want to hear it.

"I'll be gone for a couple of months. Maybe more." He nodded toward his house. "I'll find someone to look after the place."

I could see his mind was made up.

"Let me know if you need anything," I said.

He offered a thank-you and the best smile he could manage under the circumstances, and I headed for Main Street.

Had I done the right thing? I asked myself. Should I have told Mitch about Caitlin's doubts? And even if I had, would it have made any difference?

If Mitch acted on my words, if he went to Caitlin and professed his love for her, would she want that? Or would it make her life even more difficult? If she knew how he felt, but still felt obligated to marry Scott, would anyone be any better off?

When I reached Main Street I stopped on the corner, thinking. Maybe I'd done the right thing staying out of the situation with Mitch and Caitlin.

One thing I couldn't stay out of was Eleanor's murder investigation.

My suspect list was short—and filled with holes. Still, what I had, the little I had, was solid.

Rayna, Eleanor's niece, had both motive and opportunity. She was set to inherit Eleanor's house, which she desperately needed. She'd argued with Eleanor the morning she was killed. Easily, she could have gone to the visitor center and murdered her. My unanswered questions were simple ones—where had she gotten the shears engraved with my name, and why had she wanted to implicate me in the murder?

Kendall held a spot on my suspect list, simply because she'd been there that morning. My reasoning was thin but seemed more meaningful after I'd learned she'd suddenly left town, and nobody seemed to know where she'd gone. After visiting her house, I doubted she'd ever come back. I couldn't imagine Kendall would want to frame me for Eleanor's murder—we'd always gotten along well—but maybe she held a grudge I didn't know about. As with Rayna, how had she gotten my personalized shears?

Mona was definitely a suspect—even the sheriff thought so, apparently. She and Eleanor had tangled more than once, to the point where they'd threatened each other. And, of course, there was that mysterious *incident* in Mona's past.

Gloria, of course, was on my suspect list. I'd put her there because of her absence from the visitor center that morning, which wasn't much of a reason. But now, after she'd told Harriet those lies about my involvement with the lost wallets, I wondered if she'd hated me all along. Had she somehow gotten her hands on my shears to point a finger at me?

Helen had a confrontation with Eleanor. She'd seemed evasive when I'd spoken with her yet was sure she'd eventually be implicated in the murder because she'd been a witness who hadn't come forward. There were lots of questions concerning Helen's behavior. I decided it was time to get some answers.

When I got to the bank, a few customers were in the teller line, everybody speaking in a whisper. Mr. Jarvis, seated at his desk, gave me a sharp look before turning back to his computer. Helen was even less glad to see me.

"I knew you'd come back," she hissed as I stood in front of her desk. "Come on."

As before, I followed her through the bank, down the hallway, and out the back door into the parking lot. A couple approached and got into their car parked nearby. Helen waited until they drove away.

"You kept checking around, didn't you?" she snapped. "I knew you would."

I hadn't but I wasn't going to say so.

Helen huffed. "All right. Fine. I'll tell you. I was at a job interview."

"That morning? The morning Eleanor was murdered?" I asked. "That's the reason you were at the government center?"

"You don't know what it's like working here." Helen nodded toward the bank. "Everything I do is scrutinized. Mr. Jarvis is always on me, watching, just waiting for me to screw up something. Do you have any idea what that's like?"

Actually, it reminded me of the job I'd had in Los Angeles. Not a good memory.

"Dealing with customers." Helen pulled a pack of cigarettes from the pocket of her jacket. "Unreasonable. Always wanting special consideration. I couldn't do what they wanted—but I had to be nice about it. I didn't dare offend a customer, no matter how ridiculous their demands."

Helen pulled a cigarette from the pack and held it between two fingers. "It's a terrible position to be in, and worse when somebody threatens you."

"Threatens to go over your head to Mr. Jarvis?" I asked.

"That happened every day," Helen said, as if it were nothing. "I'm talking about threats. Real threats."

I hadn't thought banking would be dangerous.

"What kind of threats?" I asked.

Helen put the cigarette to her lips for a few seconds, as if thinking, then pulled it away.

"Okay, look. I'll tell you because I know you're having the same problem," she said.

Great. Another rumor in town about me.

"I know Gloria is trying to get you fired from the visitor center," she said. "She's been in the bank over and over, wanting me to waive the late charges on her credit cards and the overdraft fees on her checking account."

"Why would she expect you'd do that?"

Helen squared her shoulders and drew herself up a little.

"It's just for recreation," she told me. "Relaxation. That's it. Nothing serious. I mean, I'm by no means a compulsive gambler."

I remembered then that Marissa had mentioned her grandmother had seen Gloria at the casino over in Elliot. Helen had been there, too?

"But you know how Gloria can be," Helen went on. "She can twist things around, lie about things, and make it all seem worse than it really is. She threatened to tell Mr. Jarvis she'd seen me there."

"He'd care that you went to a casino?"

"Care?" Helen's eyes widened. "He'd fire me."

My eyes popped open wider, too.

"You don't understand my position here," she said. "Gambling is a huge no-no for employees of financial institutions. I have access to the vault. I oversee the tellers. I'm authorized to sign checks and to approve loan requests. Tens of thousands of dollars are at my fingertips. If Mr. Jarvis had an inkling that my behavior was suspect, that there were any integrity issues, he'd get rid of me."

"And Gloria knew that?" I asked.

"Oh, yes. She sure did. That was her leverage to get me to waive all her fees," Helen said.

"Gloria was blackmailing you," I realized.

"Then, somehow, Eleanor found out, and she insisted I go to Mr. Jarvis and confess. It was the right thing to do, she told me. I should clear the air, she said."

So that explained the confrontation I'd heard about between Helen and Eleanor.

"Easy for her to say, she wasn't trying to hold on to a job. As miserable as this place can be, I need to work. I need my paycheck," Helen said. "And if Mr. Jarvis fired me, the whole town would find out and I'd never get a responsible, high-paying job again."

"That's why you didn't come forward the morning of Eleanor's murder," I said. "You didn't want it to get back to Mr. Jarvis that you were looking for another job."

"I couldn't take it anymore. I had to do *something*." A flicker of compassion showed on Helen's face. "I hope you never have to know what that feels like."

Helen hurried back into the bank, leaving me standing in the parking lot. I knew what it was like to worry about keeping your job. The prospect of having no money, no way to pay my bills, unsure if I could keep a roof over my head. I'd been lucky Aunt Sarah took me in when I'd found myself in that position.

And here I was, in that same position again.

Thanks to Gloria.

Tomorrow, when I reported for my shift at the visitor center, Harriet might tell me to leave, to not come back. I'd be without a steady income, my life in limbo again.

Maybe I couldn't solve Eleanor's murder, but I could get to the bottom of the problem with Lois's lost wallet. If I could prove Gloria wrong, I could save my job.

All I had to do was get inside that luxe cabinet.

And I had to do it tonight.

CHAPTER 23

Helen murdered Eleanor.

I knew it. I was absolutely convinced I had found Eleanor's killer. The scenario had played over and over in my head since this afternoon when I'd talked to Helen outside the bank. I focused my thoughts on it now—easier than thinking about what I was about to do.

Breaking and entering wasn't actually a crime if you had a key, right? I hoped not.

I'd waited in my bedroom until after eleven o'clock, made sure Aunt Sarah was sleeping, then slipped out of the house. There was no moon tonight. The streetlamps glimmered faintly. Few windows shone in the houses I passed.

I'd dressed in black and put my hair up in a bun—I don't know why, really, it just made me feel stealthier. Now, slipping through the shadows along Main Street, I made my way toward the visitor center. Inside my tote bag were the tools I'd need to break into the luxe cabinet, as suggested by the YouTube videos I'd watched, and find out what was up with Lois's missing wallet.

I needed to keep my job. Helen needed to keep hers, too. She'd told me Eleanor had insisted she go to Mr. Jarvis and confess her trips to the casino, claiming it was the right thing to do, and she should clear the air. It sounded innocent enough, but was it?

Had it gone further? Had Eleanor threatened to go to Mr. Jarvis herself? She'd threatened to report Mona's yard to the mayor's office; it wasn't a stretch to think she'd done the same to Helen.

A few lights were on inside the government center offices as I approached the visitor center. I huddled in the shadows and surveyed the area. Not a person was in sight. Not a single car cruised by. I darted across the street and circled the building to the rear entrance of the visitor center.

Security lighting illuminated the few vehicles scattered across the parking lot. Nobody was around. I fished the key out of my tote, mentally rehearsing my plan. Get inside, go directly to the luxe cabinet, open it, check the contents, then get out.

Simple—except that my heart was pounding and my hands shook.

With a final glance around, I unlocked the door, slipped inside, and closed it behind me.

Feeble overhead lights lit the storage room making the clutter and chaos of the boxes, fixtures, and supplies seem ominous. I thought of Eleanor and the morning she'd been murdered in this very room. Anyone could be hiding in here, lying in wait, even now.

I gave myself a mental shake, reminded myself of my plan, and headed down the most direct route through the clutter toward the office.

A voice boomed from behind me. "Hold it right there!"

I jumped and spun around. The light was dim and most of

the storage room was in shadows. I made out the shape of a large man standing in the doorway, outlined by the light in the parking lot beyond.

"Don't move!" He stepped closer, into the light, and I saw that it was Sheriff Grumman.

A little groan rattled in my throat.

He spoke into the radio on his shoulder and walked toward me.

"Keep your hands where I can see them."

I moved forward a little until I was beneath one of the room's few light fixtures.

"It's me," I said lamely. "Abbey Chandler."

Behind him, Owen appeared in the doorway, followed a few seconds later by Zack. The sheriff had called for backup, apparently.

The two of them moved up beside Sheriff Grumman. I saw both their gazes sweep the scene, assessing it, then land on me.

Owen looked at Zack, threw up his hands, and left.

"What are you doing here?" the sheriff demanded.

What could I say? How would explain I was here—without telling him the truth, that I'd come here to break into the luxe cabinet.

I gulped hard. "I work here."

"At this time of night?"

"I'm the cleaning lady."

Sheriff Grumman squinted his eyes and pursed his lips. I could see he didn't believe me.

"You must have heard," I said. "It's all over town."

The sheriff paused for a few seconds, then turned to Zack.

"That true?" Sheriff Grumman asked.

Zack stared at me. He placed his hands on his gun belt and

drummed his fingers against the leather. My heart pounded. I held my breath.

What felt like six months passed and, finally, Zack nodded.

"Yeah. That's what I heard."

Sheriff Grumman eyed Zack for a moment, then turned to me again. I expected him to say something, maybe caution me about being here alone after hours, or remind me that a woman had been murdered in this very room. Instead, he left the building.

Zack stayed. He continued to glare at me, still tapping his fingertips against his gun belt. I could see he was—something. Worried, befuddled. Angry, maybe, that he'd been put on the spot with the sheriff by confirming my alibi, an alibi he knew wasn't true.

"What the hell are you doing here?" He strode closer. Angry.

I was in no mood to be yelled at.

"Cleaning!" I darted to the closet, grabbed the broom, then stalked back and shook it. "Everybody says so! It's all over town! I'm the cleaning lady!"

"Put that down."

Zack spoke in his deputy voice, as if he thought I might actually hit him with the broom. I hadn't even thought about it. But now that he'd mentioned it—

Zack grabbed the broom out of my hand and sailed it like a javelin across the storage room.

It was kind of hot.

He drew a breath, as if to calm himself. "Why are you here?"

No way was I telling him anything—especially why I was here.

"It's none of your concern," I told him.

"Actually, it is."

He was right. I knew that. But I wasn't going to admit it.

"You don't want to know," I said.

Zack paced around a bit and rubbed his forehead before turning to me again.

"Has this got something to do with Eleanor's murder?" he asked.

"That reminds me," I said, annoyed now. "You could have told me that the sheriff had a suspect—a real suspect, not just me."

"You know I can't talk about an ongoing investigation," he said.

"You could have hinted, or something."

"And you could tell me why you're really here."

We stared at each other for a few tense seconds in a stand-off, each of us determined to wait out the other.

I still didn't want to tell him the truth, so I tried some misdirection.

"I guess we need to work on our communication skills," I said.

"We sure do."

"I'm glad we're in agreement," I said. "You first."

I could see it didn't suit him, but he said, "Okay. The suspect is Mona—"

"I know."

He frowned. "How do you know?"

"You don't want to know."

His frown deepened, now even more unhappy with me. Still, he went on.

"There were several disagreements between Eleanor and Mona—"

"Yeah, yeah, the lawn controversy." I made a spinning motion with my hand. "What happened in Mona's past that makes the sheriff consider her a suspect?"

"She assaulted a coworker."

I gasped. No wonder Mona was having trouble finding a job.

"Your turn," Zack told me. "What are you doing here?"

He'd stuck his neck out, put himself in a potentially difficult position with the sheriff to cover my excuse for being here, and we'd agreed to an exchange of information. I didn't want to, but I knew I had to tell him the truth.

"I came here to break into the luxe cabinet where the expensive designer items are—"

"Stop!" Zack waved both hands. "Don't say another word."

"I told you that you didn't want to know."

He shook his head as if now he was at a complete loss about what to do or think. Knowing what he now knew, he was in an even worse spot—arrest me or walk away?

Finally, I guess he'd had enough.

"Let's go." He waved toward the door.

I'd hoped he'd leave so I could get on with the reason I came here. I could see that wasn't going to happen.

We left the storage room. Zack closed the door with a thud. I realized the key was still in my hand—not smart, since I could have dropped it and how would I have explained to Harriet why I needed a new one? I'd have to remember that the next time I broke in—which I might have to do if I couldn't figure another way to find out what was in the luxe cabinet.

Zack seemed to read my thoughts. He leaned closer, his serious deputy expression firmly in place.

"Whatever you're up to, forget about it."

He didn't wait for my response, just touched my elbow and escorted me around the building to Main Street. I thought he'd head to the sheriff's station in the government center, but he stayed by my side.

"You don't have to walk me home," I said. "It's very courteous but not necessary."

"I'm not being courteous."

"Deputies don't give personal escorts."

"I'm not doing this because it's my duty."

"Then why are you—"

I stopped because I realized why he was walking me home—to make sure I didn't go back to the visitor center. So much for trust. Yet I guess I deserved it.

We walked down Main Street in silence. Not a single car passed us. No one else was out. Not even a dog barked.

We turned onto Hummingbird Lane. The neighborhood was just as quiet.

"Does the sheriff have any more suspects in Eleanor's murder?" I asked.

"No."

He sounded tense and a little grumpy. It was my fault, of course. I guess my involvement in another crime was the last thing he wanted to talk about.

Or maybe he was rethinking his career choice.

I considered telling him about my belief that Helen had murdered Eleanor, but this, obviously, wasn't the right time. We hadn't been getting along well lately so I thought maybe I should lighten the mood.

We stopped in front of the gate in the picket fence that surrounded Aunt Sarah's house.

I tried for a playful smile. "Want to talk about sex?"

Heat exploded off him. He leaned down.

"No. I don't want to *talk* about sex. I want to—"

"Abbey?"

A voice called and a man stepped out of the shadow by the front door.

Zack pushed himself in front of me, blocking me, sheltering me from the possible threat.

"Abbey?" he called again.

"Who's there?" Zack demanded.

"Clark," he answered.

Memories of my old job in Los Angeles bloomed in my head.

I leaned around Zack.

"Clark?" I called. "Clark Connor?"

CHAPTER 24

"He's related to the Rockefellers," Anna announced.

"He must be loaded," Geraldine gushed.

"I heard he's staying in a suite at the hotel," Valerie added. "The presidential suite."

Sarah's Sweets was crowded with ladies who'd seen or heard about Clark Connor's arrival in Hideaway Grove. Seemed the town's gossip mill had been churning out rumors all morning.

"I saw what he was driving." Jodi placed a tray of warm sugar cookies on top of the display case. Aunt Sarah busied herself in the kitchen.

"Something expensive, I'll bet," Valerie said.

"I saw it, too. One of those self-driving cars. A Tesla," Anna said, helping herself to a cookie.

"Those are expensive," Geraldine declared. "He owns a chateau in France. That's what I heard."

"Then what's he doing in Hideaway Grove?" Valerie asked.

Anna bit into another cookie. "He's here looking for new

212 Dorothy Howell

business opportunities. He wants to build an office complex."

"I heard it was a shopping mall," Jodi said.

"He wants to bring new business into town. I should meet
with him." Geraldine shivered. "I hope he goes for my
rodeo idea."

"Abbey, you must know," Valerie said. "You two had a
love affair at that job you worked in Los Angeles."

"A torrid affair," Jodi added.

"He's a good-looking man," Geraldine mused. "It had to
have been a torrid affair."

Everybody looked at me, waiting.

Great. Another rumor.

"I knew Clark in Los Angeles. We worked at the same
place," I explained. "We didn't—did not—have a love affair."

"So, he's available?" Geraldine asked.

Actually, all we'd done was chat when we occasionally
ended up in the breakroom together. Clark worked in a different department; he had a middle-management position.
He'd been friendly, a welcome change from the intensity of
the department I worked in.

"I'll bet he realized how much he cared for you after you
left that job," Jodi told me. "That's why he's here."

Clark was one of those people you knew was destined for
something more, something bigger. I always felt he was bid-
ing his time, learning, gaining experience, waiting for the
right moment and opportunity to launch his life to the next
level. Had he now reached the point—and wanted to do it in
Hideaway Grove?

"I doubt he's here for me," I said.

"I guess you'll find out for sure when you two get together," Jodi said.

I didn't mention that Clark and I had lunch plans. Last night outside Aunt Sarah's house, Zack had hung around while Clark and I chatted. I'd picked up on some male posturing and witnessed the too-aggressive handshake men often did. Clark had asked me to go to lunch with him today and I'd accepted. Zack refused to leave until I went into the house. When I looked outside later, he'd stationed himself by the front gate, making sure Clark didn't return, apparently.

"The bridal show is coming up soon," Aunt Sarah announced as she approached the display case. "Lots to do today."

The ladies took the hint and left the bakery. I went into the sewing studio. The first thing I noticed, of course, was Caitlin's wedding dress hanging on the pillowcase dress rack. It was beautiful, and perfect for the occasion. But I couldn't help thinking it symbolized change—Caitlin moving into a new era in her life, Mitch leaving town, Eleanor no longer around. Things would be different in Hideaway Grove.

Would my life change as well?

Really, I didn't think for a minute that Clark had gone to the trouble of locating me, then come all the way to Hideaway Grove to pursue me romantically. Still, I'd taken a little more time with my hair and makeup this morning, and really wished I had my favorite jeans to wear. It reminded me of how long it had been since a man had invited me out.

Maybe I was due for a few changes.

A major one seemed to be headed my way, I thought, as I opened the windows. Harriet had texted me first thing this morning advising me I wouldn't be needed for my shift today at the visitor center. She hadn't fired me, but I sensed it was coming. Small consolation that it meant I wouldn't have to make those vests. But it would leave me with no way to figure out what happened to Lois's wallet. Clearing my name was important, no matter what.

I got busy with the tote bag order I'd received, the one for Brooke's bachelorette party. Thankfully, the design she'd given me was good, though I could see she'd deliberately made it simple, a reflection of her low opinion of my sewing skills.

While the embroidery machine stitched away, thoughts of Eleanor's murder floated through my brain. I was convinced Helen had killed her. She had the strongest motive I'd found—fear of losing her job.

I'd like to have thought that Eleanor had Helen's best interest at heart when she'd found out that Gloria had been blackmailing her and had insisted she report her gambling to Mr. Jarvis. I'd imagined that, again with the best of intentions, Eleanor had wanted to put a stop to the stress Helen was living under by reporting it to the bank manager herself.

Helen had admitted to being at the government center that morning. She had motive and opportunity. Still, I had to figure out how she got her hands on my personalized shears. Once I had that piece of the puzzle, I felt I had to go to Sheriff Grumman.

"Ready?" a voice behind me called.

I whirled around and saw Clark standing in the doorway. I'd been so caught up in thoughts of Eleanor's death, I'd lost all track of time.

"Sure," I said, and gathered my things.

Clark looked quite handsome, dressed in dark slacks, a dress shirt with the collar open, and a sport coat, all in complementary shades of blue. He was tall—as tall as Zack,

I thought, then wished I hadn't—with dark hair and blue eyes. I guess he was thirty, maybe a year or two older.

"So, this is where the magic happens?" Clark said, looking around the sewing studio. "Your tote bag business."

Thank goodness he hadn't heard the rumor that I was the cleaning lady.

"How'd you know?" I asked.

Clark gave me a small smile. It was a really nice smile.

"I admit, I asked around about you at the office," he said.

I stayed in touch with Madison, one of the few friends I'd made while working there. She must have told Clark what I was up to these days.

"Still, you were hard to locate," he said. "I asked around all over town. Seemed I kept missing you, so I staked out your house. I hope I didn't cause you any trouble."

"Everybody thinks you're a stalker now," I told him, and grinned.

He laughed, too. "Ready for lunch?"

We left the sewing studio and passed through the bakery with Jodi and Aunt Sarah peering at us from the kitchen. I knew they'd want a full report when I got back.

As we walked down Main Street, Clark asked if I'd like to eat in the dining room at the hotel. It was a lovely restaurant, rather elegant, but awfully close to the room he was staying in. I didn't want any more rumors going around town about me, so I suggested the Parliament Café. Nice, but more casual.

Only a few diners were inside seated in the booths and at the counter when we walked in. Melinda, one of the waitresses, was a friend of mine and a frequent volunteer at my pillowcase dress parties. She was around forty with dark hair, and looked as good as anybody possibly could in a waitress uniform.

Melinda gave me an appreciative eyebrow bob and showed us to a booth. She lingered an inordinate amount of time handing us menus, explaining the day's specials, and getting our drink order before finally leaving us alone.

"What brings you to Hideaway Grove?" I asked.

"You."

I knew he'd come here looking for me, but I couldn't imagine why. The rumors circulating that he was looking for business opportunities seemed more likely.

"You're going to have to explain," I said.

Outside, I saw Zack, in uniform, walk past the café.

"Los Angeles is in my rearview mirror," Clark said. "I'm heading up north. I'm starting my own company and I want you to be part of it."

This, I hadn't expected. Nor was I sure I wanted it, after the situation I'd found myself in at my last job.

Clark seemed to read my thoughts.

"Look, I know what happened to you. You were done wrong. That supervisor you had was terrible," he said.

Upper management had finally realized what was going on in my department, but it was too late by then. I was gone and I wasn't going back.

"I saw the potential in you," Clark said.

Through the window, I saw Zack walk past in the opposite direction.

"I want you in on the ground floor of my new venture," Clark said.

Melinda arrived with our drinks, iced teas for both of us.

"Ready to order?" She took out her order pad and pen, gazing at Clark.

"We need a few more minutes," I said.

"I don't mind waiting," she said, not taking her eyes off Clark.

Zack walked past the café again.

"I'll have the chef salad," I told Melinda.

She didn't write it down.

"And what can I get for you?" she asked Clark.

"Same."

She didn't write that down, either.

"You know," she said to Clark. "I can provide anything you'd ask for. Anything."

"Thank you, Melinda," I said. She didn't move. "*Thank you.*"

That seemed to break the spell. Melinda left.

"I'm offering you a management position," Clark said. "You're exactly what I'm looking for."

"I . . . I don't know," I said.

"Think it over, will you?" Clark asked.

Melinda peered over the counter at us. Zack strode in front of the café again.

Leave? And give up life in a small town?

Clark and I chatted through lunch. He told me what he intended to do with the marketing business he wanted to open, what his plans were, and how I'd fit in. I listened, taking it all in, determined to keep Clark the man separate from the opportunity he was offering. He paid, then walked me back to the bakery.

"You'll think about my offer?" he asked, as we stood outside.

"Of course," I said.

He gave me one last smile, which I was really starting to like, then headed down Main Street toward the hotel. I stood there for a moment, the easy vibe of Hideaway Grove drifting around me, the pleasant hum of the occasional car passing by, the chatter of tourists and locals as they strolled past.

"You'd better watch out for that guy." Zack appeared next to me, frowning as he delivered his dire warning. "I don't trust him."

"I saw you holding off that crime wave in front of the café," I said.

"It's mighty convenient he just shows up like this," he insisted. "I get a bad vibe from him. He's up to something."

"Like what?"

"Something." He paused. "You shouldn't get involved with him. He's facing arrest."

"For what?" I demanded.

"I haven't decided yet."

Good grief. Men.

Across the street, Caitlin waved from the pet store entrance, then jogged over.

"Am I interrupting something?" she asked, picking up on the look I'd just given Zack.

"No," I told her. "He's leaving."

Caitlin and I went into the bakery. Jodi looked up from the work island in the kitchen.

"I want details!" she called.

"I just need her for a minute, then she's all yours," Caitlin said.

"What's up?" I asked, as we headed toward the sewing studio.

"I want to thank you for our talk about the wedding," she said. "I was upset and stressed, and not sure what to do. You were so sweet to listen and help me get through it. Because I know now that marrying Scott is the right thing to do."

"Oh," I said, a little surprised. "Well, good. Glad to hear it."

"I mean, it's all set. Everything is in place. What could go wrong?"

We walked into the sewing studio. Caitlin's wedding dress was half off the hanger. Cheddar crouched on the skirt, hissing, howling, and clawing. Tufts of lace, shreds of fabric, rows of beads and crystals were strewn everywhere, floating in the air, littering the floor.

Caitlin screamed.

CHAPTER 25

Caitlin screamed.

I screamed.

Lily dashed into the sewing studio and screamed.

Aunt Sarah and Jodi rushed in. They screamed.

Zack charged in, ready for action.

"What the . . . ?" Zack looked at us, completely befuddled, his gaze sweeping the room desperate to determine what had us all in such a state. "What's wrong? What happened?"

We all spoke at once, a cacophony of shrill, high-pitched voices, accompanied by wringing hands and expressions of horror.

"My . . . my dress!" Caitlin managed to shriek.

Zack saw it then, in shreds, Cheddar frantically digging his claws into the delicate fabric.

Zack reached for his gun. "You want me to shoot the cat?"

"No!" we all screamed in unison.

Cheddar raced to Zack, clawed his pant leg, then sailed out the window.

Caitlin stared at the remains of her wedding dress, too overwhelmed to speak. We were all stunned, frozen in a horrified tableau, as if trying to comprehend what had happened.

Zack slammed the window, breaking the spell.

"Oh, Caitlin . . ." Jodi moaned.

Aunt Sarah couldn't seem to form a single word.

Really, what could anyone say at a time like this?

I took Caitlin's arm gently. "We should go."

She didn't respond, didn't budge, just continued to stare at the remains of her wedding dress.

"Maybe a beer at the Night Owl?" I suggested.

"No! You can't," Lily told me.

Lily? What was she doing here?

She glanced at the faces around us, stunned in a different way now.

"No, Abbey, you can't do that. There's someplace you have to go," she insisted.

I had no idea what had gotten into Lily, but I couldn't abandon my best friend in her time of extraordinary distress.

"I have to take Caitlin—"

"Like we said. Remember?" Lily hopped up and down and pointed toward the door. "You have to *go!* Now!"

It hit me then.

"You mean—"

"Yes," she told me. "*Go!*"

I grabbed Caitlin's arm. "You're coming with me."

"Is it ruined?" Caitlin asked.

"I'm afraid so," I said.

"Destroyed? Completely?"

"Yep."

"Beyond hope?" she asked.

She was asking for my opinion more as a way to try to come to terms with what had happened to her wedding dress. I saw no reason to hold back.

"Unsalvageable," I told her.

"Mom is going to be devastated."

We were in my car heading for Hero's Bar in Holden. Of all the times for Lily to show up, wanting me to catch Owen in the act of cheating on Willow, it couldn't have happened at a worse moment. Still, I was glad to get Caitlin out of there. Continuing to fixate on her ruined dress wouldn't have done her any good.

We rode the rest of the way in silence—really, what could we possibly talk about?

The two-lane road had been built decades ago and was now considered the back way to Holden. It wound through a largely rural area. Houses were few and far between. We passed only a couple of cars. Most everyone took the free-way to Holden—unless, of course, like Owen, they didn't want to be seen driving through Hideaway Grove, trying to leave unnoticed.

Finally, my GPS announced we'd reached our destina-tion. I spotted the Hero's Bar and Grill off to the left, stand-ing alone amid a gravel parking lot already accommodating about a dozen cars and pickups. Neon signs burned in the windows.

I turned into the lot. My tires crunched on the gravel as I circled to the rear of the building. Dumpsters sat across from the back door; wooden pallets were stacked nearby. Several vehicles were parked there. One of them was Owen's truck, purposefully left there, out of sight, hiding.

Can't say I was glad to see it, despite Lily's insistence that I catch him with another woman and put an end to her sus-picion. I'd secretly wished he wouldn't be here, that I wouldn't have to confront him, that I wouldn't have a hand in breaking Willow's heart.

Too late for that now.

I drove to the front of the building, pulled into a parking space, and killed the engine.

Caitlin looked at the sign lit in neon colors. "Why are we here?"

I'd explained our mission to her as we'd left Hideaway Grove, but she'd been too upset to comprehend. I told her again what was going on. I still wasn't sure she grasped the situation.

We left the car and crossed the parking lot. I mentally braced myself, ready to handle coming face-to-face with Owen and whomever he was cheating with.

I'd had a couple of women in mind, but now, in this moment, it was hard to imagine I was right. Would one of them knowingly involve herself with Owen, fully aware of how he and Willow had been committed to each other for so long? And how could Owen do such a thing? Sneak around, cheat, treat Willow so shabbily?

My anger started to build as I walked into the bar, Caitlin behind me. The room was large, dimly lit, and furnished with a row of booths along one wall, pool tables and dartboards on the opposite side, and tables scattered in between. About half of the seating was occupied by customers, casually dressed. The bar ran across the rear of the room, fronted with stools and backed by a mirror and shelves of liquor bottles. A jukebox played a song I didn't recognize.

I spotted Owen right away standing next to the last booth in the row where a dark-haired woman sat. She looked up at him, smiling, and laughed.

I felt like I'd been punched.

Crossing the room in long strides, I planted myself next to him.

"Hi, Owen." I shouted at him, my voice filled with rage and accusation.

He turned to me, and a big smile bloomed on his face. "Abbey, what a surprise. I haven't seen you in here before."

I looked pointedly at the woman seated in the booth, then at Owen again. "And I'm sure you weren't expecting me."

Now he looked sheepish. "I guess you're surprised to see me here."

"I sure am," I told him. "You want to explain yourself?"

"Busted." He sighed. "I figured this would happen sooner or later."

I was even more angry now. He'd been caught, and he acted as if it were nothing.

"Let me get you something." Owen motioned toward the bar. "How about a beer?"

"Make it two," the woman in the booth said. "No, three."

I noticed then that another woman sat across from her. They were both a little older than I'd initially thought, maybe in their fifties.

"Coming up," Owen said.

Caitlin, behind me, tapped me on the shoulder.

Owen circled around behind the bar and patted the spot on the end.

"Have a seat," he said to me.

He grabbed two bottles of beer and two chilled mugs from the cooler and placed them on the table for the ladies.

Caitlin tapped my shoulder again.

"Bottle or draft?" Owen asked me.

My anger drained away, replaced by the realization of what I was seeing.

"Abbey?" Caitlin mumbled.

"You work here," I said to Owen. "You're tending bar."

"Yep. As often as they'll have me," he said.

My cheeks heated, my breath got short. I felt like an idiot.

"I thought . . . Lily thought . . . that is, well, Willow—"

"Is she okay?" he demanded, worried. "Did something happen to her?"

"No, no, she's fine."

"Abbey?" Caitlin tugged on my arm, harder now.

"Can you keep my secret?" Owen asked. "I know it's a lot to ask. But Willow's got her heart set on an engagement ring that's pretty pricey. I've got to get it for her."

My heart melted a little. "And you're working here to make extra money so you can buy it for her?"

"She deserves it."

"Abbey!" Caitlin grabbed my arm, whirled me around, and pointed across the bar.

Scott sat at a table. Cuddled against him while he brushed kisses across her cheek was Tristin Terry.

Tristin spotted Caitlin. Her eyes widened, her mouth popped open. She lurched out of her chair so fast it fell over backward. Scott looked up and saw Caitlin. He rose slowly to his feet.

Tristin rounded the table and charged toward us. I'd never been in a bar fight, but I was sure that's what was about to happen.

Instead, Tristin stopped in front of Caitlin and tears pooled in her eyes.

"I'm sorry, Caitlin. I'm so sorry," she said.

"I'm sorry, too." Scott stepped up beside Tristin, solemn, sincere. "I'm sorry you found out this way, Caitlin."

"We didn't mean for this to happen," Tristin said, and swiped away her tears. "But when I moved back to Hide-away Grove and we saw each other, the feelings we had for each other in high school came rushing back."

"I should have told you a long time ago, right from the

start," Scott said. "But everybody was so caught up in us getting married, my folks, your folks. I'd made a commitment to you. I didn't know how to back out of it."

Caitlin stared at him, as if in a trance.

"I did you wrong. I deserve your anger," Scott said. "Whatever you need to say to me, go ahead."

Caitlin threw her arms around him. "Thank you!"

CHAPTER 26

"You're okay with this?" I asked.

Caitlin didn't hesitate. "I am."

We were seated side by side in the sewing studio, shears in our hands, the remains of her wedding dress spread across our laps.

"You first," I told her.

She drew a cleansing breath and smiled—actually smiled, the first genuine smile I'd seen on her face in a very long time—and cut into the fabric of her wedding dress.

"You're okay?" I asked again, just to make sure.

"I am."

"How'd it feel?"

"Freeing."

Convinced now that Caitlin was really okay with what we were doing, I started in on the dress myself.

It had been her idea to salvage the lace, pearls, crystals, and anything else possible, and use them to embellish the pillowcase dresses. She'd appeared in the sewing studio first thing this morning and told me. It was incredibly generous of her, especially under the circumstances.

"How's your mom holding up?" I asked.

"Still upset this morning, but she's coming to terms with it."

After Scott's confession at the Hero's Bar yesterday, we'd driven back to Hideaway Grove. When I'd dropped her off, she'd told me her intention to tell her mom right away, even though she was still trying to come to terms with the dramatic, life-changing event she'd just been through. I'd agreed. Better her mom heard it from Caitlin and not from the rumor destined to blast through Hideaway Grove like a water cannon.

"And your dad?" I asked.

"She hasn't told him yet."

We snipped away, creating embellishments that would enhance the pillowcase dresses. I'd expected Lily to come by this morning, too. I'd called her yesterday, sworn her to absolute secrecy—no way was I ruining Owen's surprise after all his hard work—and explained what he was doing for Willow. She'd cried with relief.

"What are you going to do now, since the wedding is off?" I asked.

"I have a few ideas. I need to work out the details," Caitlin said. "I heard about the mystery man who'd showed up in town, looking for you."

"Clark Connor. We used to work at the same place in L.A.," I said. "He offered me a job."

"That's it? Nothing romantic going on?"

"Nope," I said.

"Are you going to take the job? Will you have to leave Hideaway Grove?"

I hadn't thought his proposal over in detail, with everything that I'd been dealing with. But maybe his timing was good, especially since, once again, Harriet had cancelled my shift at the visitor center today.

"Hello?" Rayna stood at the pocket doors. "Are you up for some company?"

"Sure," I said.

Rayna had been on my mental suspect list, a person likely to have murdered Eleanor, but at the moment she looked exhausted and worn down, as if she hardly had it in her to shoo away a fly.

"I heard about what happened." She walked over and saw us snipping away with the shears. "I guess the rumor's true."

"Feel free to tell everyone you see," Caitlin said. "And let them know I'm okay with it."

"You're not mad?" Rayna asked. "I mean, after what those two did?"

Scott and Tristin were destined to bear the brunt of the gossip, understandably so. It helped that Caitlin wasn't encouraging it.

"It worked out the way it was supposed to," Caitlin said.

Rayna nodded and seemed to understand.

"So, look, I've been meaning to talk to you," she said, a note of concern in her voice. "I've seen Peri working in the pet store a lot since your dad's been sick. Did you tell her? Warn her? Does she . . . know?"

"Know what?" I asked.

"I explained everything to her the very first day she was there," Caitlin said.

"Good," Rayna said. "Because you know . . ."

"Know what?" I asked again.

Rayna and Caitlin shared a troubled look, then both of them shrugged as if coming to a mutual agreement.

"A certain someone is known for shoplifting," Caitlin said.

"Who?" I asked.

"It makes me sick looking at those shears," Rayna said.

She pointed to the ones Caitlin and I were using, the ones engraved with my name that Gloria had donated.

"Gloria?" I asked, stunned.

"All the merchants know, and we watch out for her when she shops," Caitlin explained.

"But nobody told the sheriff?" I asked.

"It's one of Hideaway Grove's best-kept secrets," Caitlin explained.

This town had kept a secret?

"Out of respect for Gloria's husband," Caitlin went on. "Reggie was always doing so much for the town. It didn't seem worth it to upset him. Gloria was more like, well, like a minor inconvenience."

"Hardly a minor inconvenience to me. She almost got me fired," Rayna declared. "Those shears. They were a special order because of the engraving. Ordinary shears wouldn't do. I was supposed to make Gloria pay in full when she ordered them, but she insisted she'd pay when she picked them up. Then she stole them—right out of our stockroom, and never paid for them. She just sneaked in there and took them. And I got the blame for it because I was supposedly not watching her."

I looked down at the shears in my hand, then at Rayna again.

"You're sure it was Gloria who took them?" I asked.

"Positive. She's the only one who knew they'd been ordered, the only one who knew they'd arrived and were in the stockroom," Rayna said. "And they were expensive. Top quality. Five pairs, personally engraved."

"Five pairs?" I asked, confused. "You're sure?"

"Absolutely," Rayna told me. "I was afraid I was going to have to reimburse the store for them—on top of being fired."

Rayna kept talking but my thoughts shot off in another direction.

Five pairs of shears had been ordered, received, and stolen from Birdie's Gifts and Gadgets's stockroom. I had three of them in my sewing studio. A fourth pair had been used to murder Eleanor.

Where was the fifth pair?

Jodi stepped into the sewing studio, smiling. "Anybody want to taste-test something new?"

"That sounds really good," Rayna said, as if welcoming the opportunity.

"I think I've had enough of this for one day." Caitlin pushed the wedding dress off her lap and laid the shears aside.

I followed them into the bakery but went into the kitchen instead of to the display case where Jodi was offering samples of the latest creation, mini tarts filled with vanilla cream and topped with strawberries. Aunt Sarah was at the work island assembling ingredients for cupcakes.

"I just heard a rumor," I said to Aunt Sarah.

"Always plenty of those going around." She smiled, then saw the serious expression on my face. "What's wrong?"

"Did you know that Gloria was a known shoplifter?" I asked.

"Oh, sure." Aunt Sarah waved away my concern. "All the merchants know."

"Looks like we've got another winner." Jodi walked into the kitchen and held out the tray with one last tart on it. "Saved you one, Abbey."

I thought about my favorite jeans, no closer to fitting like they used to. Still, the tart had fruit on it—that made it healthy, right?

I popped it into my mouth and sighed. "Delicious."

"That makes it unanimous," Jodi declared.

"You know to watch Gloria when she comes in?" I asked Aunt Sarah.

"I'm not concerned," she said. "Gloria seldom comes into the bakery. In fact, I don't think she's been in here for over a month or more."

"Just once," Jodi commented, as she rinsed the tray. "Week before last, I guess it was, when she dropped off those pillow-cases for Abbey."

Aunt Sarah frowned. "I don't remember."

"Early morning, first thing, just as I'd unlocked the door," Jodi explained. "She was in and out in a flash."

"Got to run," Caitlin called.

She and Rayna waved and left the bakery. Aunt Sarah and Jodi turned their attention to the cupcakes. I stood there, thinking.

At some point over the past week or so, I'd realized I had more pillowcases than I expected.

At the pillowcase dress party, Anna was certain some of the pillowcases I'd laid out were those that had disappeared from her stockroom.

Had Gloria taken them from Anna's store—stolen them—brought them here, and dropped them off in my sewing studio? Was she expecting more accolades for donating the super-nice pillowcases, as she'd gotten when she'd presented the volunteers with the shears engraved with my name? Shears she'd also stolen?

But Gloria had never mentioned to me that she'd brought in the pillowcases. In fact, from what Jodi said, it seemed that Gloria had made a point of coming by early for a quick drop-off, almost as if she didn't want anybody to know she'd been here.

An icy wave shot through me causing me to gasp softly.

Which morning had Gloria come by, used the pretense of making a donation, gone into my sewing studio alone, then rushed out? Which morning was that?

I thought I knew.

Gloria lived on Blue Bird Lane in a house painted pale peach, surrounded by a lovely yard and a white picket fence, like most every other house in town. A lot of love had been put into the home, I could see as I walked up, but it was showing signs of neglect. A few weeds, a loose board, shrubs that should have been trimmed several weeks ago. It seemed Gloria had let the place go, after her husband's death.

She had other priorities, if what I suspected was true.

Pausing at the front gate, I glanced around. The neighborhood was quiet; neighborhoods were always quiet in Hideaway Grove. Across the street an older man shuffled along with a beagle, who seemed to be shuffling as well. Down the block, two moms were standing on the sidewalk, both with a baby on their hip, swaying to a rhythm only new mothers seemed to feel.

I went through the gate and onto the front porch and rang the bell. I knew Gloria wasn't home. Harriet had cancelled my shift at the visitor center today because Gloria was on the schedule; obviously, Harriet didn't want to deal with the two of us working together. I waited, rang again just for show, then circled around to the rear of the house.

The backyard showed the same signs of neglect as the front, nothing major, just a slow decline. I glanced around, saw no neighbors in the adjoining yards watching, and climbed the steps to the back door.

If what I suspected was true, that meant I'd been wrong about all my other murder suspects. Rayna, Helen, Mona, though having good reasons to have killed Eleanor, were innocent. Gloria had murdered her.

It was useless to question her. She'd deny everything. If I told Sheriff Grumman what I suspected, who knew when— or if—he'd act on it.

I needed proof. Evidence. If Gloria was guilty, if she'd

murdered Eleanor, I figured the only place I'd find something incriminating was inside her house.

As long as I could get inside.

The tool kit I'd assembled to break into the luxe cabinet—courtesy of an oh-so-helpful YouTube video—was still in my tote bag. I would hardly look like a smooth operator standing here on Gloria's porch, fumbling with tools while rewatching a video on my phone, but luckily, I had another idea.

Almost every resident in Hideaway Grove kept an extra house key under a flowerpot on their back porch. Gloria didn't disappoint.

I wasn't exactly breaking and entering, since I had the key, but trespassing came to mind. I wasn't sure, and I couldn't ask anyone—certainly not Zack; he was a real stickler about enforcing laws, which I occasionally found slightly annoying.

I glanced around one last time.

Now or never, I decided.

I slid the key into the lock and went inside Gloria's home.

CHAPTER 27

The layout of Gloria's house was the same as I'd seen in most every other home in Hideaway Grove. A mudroom, the kitchen, a dining room that opened into the living room, and a hallway that led to a bathroom situated between two bedrooms. Typical, except there was an empty feel to Gloria's place, almost as if no one lived here. Still, silent. Kind of creepy.

In the kitchen, no dirty dishes sat in the sink, the countertops were free of crumbs, the trash can wasn't running over. The appliances seemed to be original to the house, as did the flooring and the fixtures.

The dining table and six chairs sported a fine layer of dust. A recliner sat in the corner of the living room. A strip of duct tape covered what must have been a rip in the fabric of one of the arms—Reggie's favorite chair, probably. It faced a TV on a wooden stand, with a shelf underneath that held what I thought was a VCR player.

I wasn't sure how long I'd been here, but my anxiety level was increasing, telling me I needed to hurry.

The hardwood floor creaked as I walked down the hallway. On the right I spotted Gloria's bedroom. The bed was unmade, the closet door stood open, shoes and clothing were scattered across the floor and draped across the chest and dresser. The room felt closed up, stuffy; it smelled like Gloria.

I hadn't spotted any evidence that would incriminate Gloria in Eleanor's murder, nothing lying around, no evidence casually tossed aside. I was certain Eleanor's death wasn't Gloria's only crime, and if I didn't find it in the second bedroom, I didn't know where else to look.

I crossed the hall. This bedroom was in far better shape, I saw when I stepped inside. The bed, chest, and nightstands looked old, like everything else in the house, but seemed to have suffered less wear. A small desk sat in the corner with a computer surrounded by scattered papers and notes, and dozens of ink pens jammed into a coffee cup.

The bed was neatly made, which caused the ivory throw that spread across the center of it to look out of place. It was lifted in places, bunched in others. My heart rate picked up.

I pulled back the throw. Under it, among the jumble of items, was an array of wallets, cosmetic cases, and accessories all with designer labels. One of the wallets was in the distinctive Burberry print, embroidered with the initials "LTA."

Lois Atwater's wallet.

"Gotcha," I murmured.

Here it was, proof that Gloria had lied about returning Lois's wallet, proof that she'd kept it for herself—stolen it. I'd been right. My job at the visitor center was saved.

Some of the other things laid out on the bed matched the description of reported missing items I'd seen listed in Gloria's convoluted luxe log. Lois's wallet wasn't the first one Gloria had taken; she'd been at this for a while. Likely, there was nothing inside the luxe cabinet.

Among the heap of items, I spotted coffee mugs, figurines, costume jewelry, pens, a flowerpot, commemorative spoons, all sold at various stores in Hideaway Grove. And there, sticking out from under a decorative set of measuring cups—from Sarah's Sweets, I was sure—was a pair of shears, engraved with my name. The fifth pair, stolen from Birdie's Gifts and Gadgets, unaccounted for until now.

Gloria had gotten away with her crime spree by lying, bullying, and threatening others. Though nothing here pointed to her as Eleanor's murderer, I wasn't going to let this evidence lie unreported to the sheriff.

I pulled out my cell phone, tapped the video feature, and started recording. I shot the room, establishing that I was inside the bedroom in Gloria's house, then focused on the stolen items. I went slowly, taking my time, making sure to capture images of everything from multiple angles. I paid special attention to the shears.

The hardwood floors creaked behind me.

I turned and saw Gloria standing in the doorway.

Had she gotten off early from the visitor center? Or had I lost all track of time?

"I can't say I'm surprised," she said, looking unconcerned that she'd discovered me in her bedroom and that I'd uncovered her cache of stolen items.

She was dressed in an attractive pantsuit, teal, with matching pumps. A purse and tote bag—both designer items—were looped over her shoulder. Her hair and nails were done. The look made her appear poised, pulled together, and competent.

I knew differently.

"You took these things." I gestured to the items on the bed. "From stores, right here in Hideaway Grove."

Gloria walked past me to the bed and smiled. "My collection. It's impressive, isn't it."

"It's stealing," I told her. "You kept all the expensive items that were turned in to the visitor center. Kept them for yourself. That's Lois Atwater's Burberry wallet right there."

Gloria opened the closet door, rifled through the shelves, and pulled out a large tote bag. "Burberry is one of my favorites."

Gloria picked up the wallet, looked it over, and dropped it into her tote bag.

"You shipped her a knockoff, thinking she wouldn't know the difference," I said. "You forgot hers was personalized with her initials."

"This little discovery you think you've made," Gloria said, still sounding untroubled. "It means nothing. You could have staged this. You broke into my house. I found you here going through my belongings. You could have brought all these things with you, to make me look guilty."

My confidence faltered. Gloria's ease of lying, her ongoing practice of deflecting the truth, could turn this situation around, easily making me look guilty.

"You are guilty," I told her.

"Well, yes, of course I am." She gave me a smug smile. "Tourists . . . so careless. Shopping, laughing, not paying attention. Carrying those satchels, not zipping them closed. In a crowd, I could reach right in and take their wallets or whatever. I kept some, sold some along with the items that were turned in to the visitor center—the nice ones, of course. Some on eBay, others at pawn shops and consignment stores outside of Hideaway Grove."

That explained the times I'd seen her with a tote bag full of shipping boxes headed for the post office, and her absences from town that other people had mentioned.

"But so what? Who's going to believe you—or even care what I've done." Gloria selected more items from the trove and dropped them into her tote bag. "That's the beauty of it. Don't you see? People believe me."

"Every merchant in town knows you're a compulsive shoplifter," I told her.

"Rumors." Gloria continued to load her tote bag. "I have a sterling reputation in this town."

"That your husband cultivated, not you."

"Reggie." Gloria growled. "Oh, the way I had to live because of that man."

"He was very generous," I said.

"Generous? You call that generous?" Gloria's anger rose. "Look at this place! Look how I had to live! All because Reggie insisted on doing so much for others. He had no consideration for me, what I wanted. Looking good to the town, helping others—that's what he cared about."

"That's why you raised the rent on all your properties," I said.

"Why shouldn't I?" she exclaimed. "Those people hadn't paid a dime more in rent for years."

"You forced Helen to waive your late fees at the bank," I added.

"It was hardly my fault she was a gambler and I'd happened to see her at the casino. What did she expect?"

"And Reggie's will? You forged a new one."

"I had to," Gloria declared. "He'd gone behind my back and left a large chunk of our estate to those nephews of his. That money should go to me—not them."

If Gloria wondered how I knew these things, she gave no indication. It seemed she was glad to finally talk about how she'd been done wrong. Stealing and lying were bad enough. But I suspected she'd gotten away with something worse, much worse.

"How does Eleanor fit into this?" I asked.

"Eleanor." Gloria spoke the name as if it tasted sour on her lips. "Eleanor and her nosy ways. Her insistence on interfering where she wasn't wanted or needed. That woman, she actually followed me to the casino."

At least now I knew how Eleanor had learned about Helen's gambling problem; she'd seen her there at the casino while spying on Gloria.

"Eleanor approached me—right there on the gaming floor," Gloria said. "Told me I needed help. Wanted me to go to some sort of gamblers' meeting."

"That wasn't all she found out about, was it?" I said. "She knew about the things you were stealing."

Gloria shook her head slowly. "If she'd only minded her own business. Bad enough she was organizing my own renters against me, encouraging my sister-in-law to sue me, trying to get Helen to confess to Mr. Jarvis rather than waive my bank fees."

"She didn't stop there, did she?" I said. "She knew you were stealing from the visitor center. How did she find out?"

"Pieced it together. Like you did. She volunteered there, chatted with tourists, took phone calls from women desperate to recover something, pursued it, stuck her nose in where it didn't belong," Gloria said. "She confronted me. Threatened to turn me in to the sheriff and spread the news all over town."

"You had to silence her."

Gloria smiled. "Rather clever of me, if I say so myself. I simply grabbed those pillowcases from Anna's shop, dashed into the bakery, took a pair of those shears, and left."

"You knew Eleanor was supposed to work that morning. You got to the visitor center early and confronted her."

"I tried to reason with her," Gloria insisted, gathering more items from her cache and putting them into her tote bags.

I doubted that was true. Not after the trouble she'd gone to getting the shears from my sewing studio.

"You stabbed her with the shears. Killed her," I said.

"Only because she was determined to ruin my life," Gloria said, as if it were nothing, as if it were the only sensible thing to do.

"Why did you take shears from my sewing studio?" I asked. "You had a pair of your own."

"They were part of my collection. I didn't want to lose them."

Gloria loaded the last of the stolen items into her tote bags and faced me.

"I can't let you leave," I told her.

"What are you going to do, Abbey? Knock me down? Tie me up? A woman my age, with health problems, guilty of nothing more than petty theft?" Gloria asked. "I'd sue you, of course, for damages, for the injuries I sustained. I'd win. I'm a sick person, with an addiction to shoplifting, who's recently lost her husband. Who do you think a jury would side with?"

She waited, as if daring me to do something, then lifted her chin and walked past me, out of the bedroom.

She was right. A woman her age, in questionable health. I couldn't restrain her, force her to stay.

Then I realized I didn't have to.

My phone was still in my hand, still recording.

I emailed the video to Zack, then sat down and waited for him to arrive.

CHAPTER 28

"You've done a nice job." Brooke shot me a patronizing smile, which I think she meant to be encouraging, and held up one of the tote bags I'd made for her bachelorette party. "I don't care what everybody else says, your tote bags are okay."

I didn't know what to say to that—no, actually, I knew what I wanted to say but didn't think I should.

We were in the sewing studio. Brooke had dropped by unexpectedly to check on her tote bag order. Luckily, I'd just finished embroidering the last one.

"I've been talking you up all over town," Brooke went on, her fake smile still in place. "I've been telling everybody about how I saw you working so hard as the cleaning lady at the visitor center."

Oh, my goodness. It was Brooke who'd started that rumor. She'd seen me straightening the rack of sightseeing brochures and cleaning up the coffee Marissa had spilled—and assumed the worst, of course.

"Since your little tote bag business isn't going well, it's the least I can do," Brooke told me.

"Well, nice talking to you," I said, though it wasn't, of course.

I grabbed her stack of tote bags and headed for the pocket doors.

"Wait, one more thing." Brooke caught up with me. "You know I'm having my bachelorette party at my home, and I want you to come."

I paused. Brooke was inviting me to her bachelorette party? Finally, after all this time, she was doing something nice for me?

"I already have a housekeeping staff, of course," she said. "But after seeing you in action at the visitor center, scrubbing so hard, I know you'll do a much better job with the deep cleaning I need done."

When will I ever learn?

"I'll check my calendar," I told her.

With one last plastered-on smile, Brooke took her tote bags and left the sewing studio.

I wandered to the rack where the remains of Caitlin's wedding dress still lay. We'd snipped away the delicate lace and crystals to use on the pillowcase dresses, but there was more we could salvage.

That was just earlier today, I realized. It seemed like *forever* ago, after what I'd been through at Gloria's house. Hearing her confession, learning how she felt entitled to whatever she wanted and justified in doing everything she'd done, had shaken me. Zack had showed up pretty quickly, along with the sheriff, and jumped into action. I left.

Both pairs of shears engraved with my name lay atop the remnants of Caitlin's gown, where we'd dropped them. They were nice but brought back a lot of bad memories. I wasn't sure if I'd keep them. I would, however, pay Birdie's Gifts and Gadgets for them; maybe it would help Rayna keep her job.

"Hello?"

I turned, expecting to see someone at the pocket doors, but no one was there.

"Over here." Clark stood outside, looking at me through the window. He pointed toward the bakery entrance. "I'll come around."

"Stay there," I said.

If Cheddar could do it, so could I.

I sat on the sill and swung my legs over. Clark took my hand and assisted as I stood up. Gentlemanly. Nice.

"I have a confession," Clark said. "I wasn't completely honest with you."

Different scenarios skittered through my thoughts, but, oddly, none of them were troubling. Something about Clark—his soothing voice, his handsome face, his grin that I was liking more and more every time I saw it—made me think that no matter what, I could trust him.

"I told you I came here to ask you to work for me," Clark said. "But, honestly, I want more than that. I think we'd be good together."

Was he saying what I thought he was saying?

"You mean, romantically?" I asked.

Clark grinned. "I tried flirting with you when we worked together, but you never seemed interested."

That just shows how stressed I was working at that company, if I hadn't noticed that a hot guy like Clark was interested in me.

"I thought it was just an office thing, but I couldn't stop thinking about you," he said. "I tracked you down all the way to Hideaway Grove to find out."

My heart did a quick pitter-pat. "I'm flattered."

Clark nodded to the black Tesla parked at the curb. "I

have meetings up north. I'll be back in a few days. We can talk then?"

"I'd like that."

He circled the car and opened the driver's side door, then paused and looked up and down Main Street.

"This is a nice little town. I like it," he said. "I see a lot of potential here."

My heart did a few more pitter-pats as he waved, then got into his car and drove away.

"He's leaving? Good," Zack said.

I saw him then, standing next to me. Again, my heart did its little pitter-pat, but I wasn't sure if it was because of Zack, or left over from Clark.

"I don't trust that guy," Zack said.

"I suppose that means you think I should trust you?" I asked. My heart was thumping, but for a totally different reason. "Why should I when you don't trust me?"

"I never said I didn't trust you."

"You didn't tell me the truth about what Owen was up to. You knew the sheriff had a suspect in Eleanor's murder and kept it from me," I told him. "And it's none of your business what I'm doing with Clark. But just so you know, I'm spending time with him because he asked me—unlike you, who's never even invited me to dinner."

That shut him up. He didn't say anything. I wasn't sure my words even registered with him.

Finally, he said, "Gloria's car was stopped on the freeway, heading for Los Angeles. She's in custody. With the evidence found on her and the video you made, the case against her for Eleanor's murder should be a slam dunk."

I couldn't think of anything to say, though I was glad to learn that Lois Atwater would get her treasured wallet back eventually. I spun around and went into the bakery.

Jodi and Aunt Sarah were at the work island in the kitchen, swirling chocolate icing on cupcakes.

"Abbey," Aunt Sarah called. "Before I forget, don't be surprised if you hear workmen in the house tomorrow morning. The new dryer is being delivered."

I stopped. "What?"

"The old one was in such bad shape," she said. "I had the repair guy out twice, but it was no use. Something was out of whack with the heating gizmo. It kept getting too hot—shrank two of my T-shirts and my favorite jeans. Didn't you notice?"

It really was the dryer—not me?

Finally, some good news.

"Would you like a sugar cookie?" Jodi asked. "Fresh out of the oven."

"You bet," I said, and took two.

I'd finished off both of them by the time I got into the sewing studio. An order from the gift shop chain had come in for a dozen tote bags. Nice, but I wasn't getting rich like this. I definitely had to figure out something different.

I set up the embroidery machine. By the time I'd finished two of the totes, I still hadn't come up with anything to improve my future. Fortunately, Caitlin came in distracting me.

"News to share." She stood straighter, squared her shoulders, and drew a breath. "I've hired Peri to run the pet store full-time, permanently."

"What?" I exclaimed. "But what about your dad? He always insisted you were supposed to run it."

"I explained to Dad that he'd put me in charge of the pet store, which meant he trusted my judgment," Caitlin said. "So, in my judgment, Peri was fully capable of managing the pet store and that was final."

"Wow. And he was okay with it?"

"He has to be," she said. "Because I'm leaving."

"You're—what?"

Caitlin looked stronger, less stressed than I'd ever seen her—and happier.

"I'm going to Paris," she said. "With Mitch."

I gasped. "You're—what?"

"He came over. He'd just heard . . . the news." Caitlin smiled. "He was kind of out of breath when he got there. I think he ran the whole way."

My heart melted a little, for both of them.

"We talked," she said. "We decided to give it a try, see if it works."

"And where better than in Paris," I said.

We hugged and teared up a little, both of us happy about her decision.

"You two are going to be great together," I said.

She nodded thoughtfully. "I think we are."

Caitlin left and I couldn't bear the solitude of the sewing studio any longer. I closed the windows, gathered my things, and left. Outside on Main Street, I couldn't decide where to go or what to do. Nothing seemed to suit my mood. I headed home.

My best friend was leaving Hideaway Grove. My tote bag business was going nowhere. Clark said he'd be back in a few days but, honestly, I didn't know if that would happen. I didn't know if I had my job at the visitor center. Seemed nothing in my future was certain.

As I turned onto Hummingbird Lane, Cheddar suddenly appeared beside me.

"Thanks," I said. "I can use the company."

He trotted along with me to Aunt Sarah's house, up the sidewalk to the front door.

"Sorry, I can't invite you inside," I said.

Cheddar seemed okay with it. He sat down beside a pot of blooming flowers by the front door, content.

Inside, I wasn't as content. I roamed from room to room, a dozen thoughts and ideas floating through my head. None of them seemed right. Nothing in my life seemed definite. How would I ever find my path?

The doorbell rang. I opened it. Zack stood on the porch, wearing nice pants, a dress shirt, and a jacket. Cheddar purred and rubbed against his ankle.

Zack held out a small arrangement of flowers.

"Would you like to go to dinner?"